Her Sinful Marine

A SINFUL MARINES NOVEL

Makenna Jameison

This book is a work of fiction. Names, characters, places, and incidents are the product of the author's imagination. Any resemblance to actual events, locales, or persons, living or dead, is coincidental.

Copyright © 2019 by Makenna Jameison

All rights reserved, including the right of reproduction in whole or in part in any form.

ISBN: 9781076761675

ALSO BY MAKENNA JAMEISON

ALPHA SEALS

SEAL the Deal
SEALED with a Kiss
A SEAL's Surrender
A SEAL's Seduction
The SEAL Next Door
Protected by a SEAL
Loved by a SEAL
Tempted by a SEAL
Married to a SEAL
Seduced by a SEAL
Rescued by a SEAL

SOLDIER SERIES

Christmas with a Soldier
Valentine from a Soldier
In the Arms of a Soldier
Return of a Soldier
Summer with a Soldier

Table of Contents

Chapter 1	7
Chapter 2	15
Chapter 3	21
Chapter 4	38
Chapter 5	49
Chapter 6	55
Chapter 7	70
Chapter 8	80
Chapter 9	87
Chapter 10	93
Chapter 11	101
Chapter 12	115
Chapter 13	121
Chapter 14	129
Chapter 15	136
Chapter 16	143
Chapter 17	147
Chapter 18	151
Epilogue	156
About the Author	160

Chapter 1

Melissa Ford blew out a sigh, impatiently tapping her stiletto as she waited for her new client to arrive. She glanced down at the time on her phone, mentally calculating how long she'd have to spend showing him the house before she had to rush off to her next appointment. Weekends were always the busiest for her, with back-to-back showings of properties. She understood why people preferred seeing homes on Saturday or Sunday, but this was *her* work. She didn't have time to waste on late arrivals or no-shows who couldn't even bother to tell her they weren't coming.

She walked across the porch, her heels clicking on the smooth stone, her gaze sweeping the empty street.

Not a car in sight.

So much for doing her best friend a favor. She never took on new clients first without a preliminary meeting in the office to go over everything. And this was exactly why.

Serious inquiries only.

Perching on the wrought-iron bench, she crossed her legs, the skirt of her slim suit tightening across her thighs. She worked out occasionally—nothing like her best friend, who was an avid runner—and her outfit today skimmed her curves like a glove. Amy always had said she'd kill for Melissa's hourglass figure.

Not that Melissa minded flaunting her assets.

She adjusted her suit jacket, the camisole she had on beneath hugging her full breasts. At least it wasn't ninety degrees out in the summer or something. Then she'd really be irritated. Still, she had better ways to spend her day than sitting around on the front porch of a house she needed to sell. Not when she had other showings back-to-back.

Other people waiting for her.

Melissa tried calling her client again, on the off-chance that he'd gotten lost.

In a car accident.

Attacked by zombies.

She smirked, brushing her long red hair back over her shoulder. The phone rang and rang but then went to voicemail.

Tyler Braxton had been stationed clear across the country somewhere in Colorado and had only recently moved to Quantico. He'd been renting but was looking to purchase a house here. She'd never even met the man, only dealt with him via phone and email. And maybe she never would meet him, she thought, annoyed. If he couldn't be bothered to show up or cancel, she'd move on to her other clients.

She should've known better than to agree to meet with the Marine. Her own ex-fiancé certainly had turned out to be unreliable, what with proposing to her and then up and cancelling the wedding only two months before the big day.

Guys like that were married to their careers.

Or interested in sleeping with as many women as possible.

Why should Michael tie himself down to her when there were plenty of other fish in the sea?

She smirked.

Three years wasted with him. Although Amy was happily dating her neighbor, Jason, who happened to be stationed at Quantico as well, he seemed to be the anomaly.

The rest of them were all assholes.

Fifteen minutes later, a large black SUV pulled up to the curb, and a burly Marine who had to be none other than Tyler stepped out. He was at least six-foot-two, with cropped blond hair and aviators concealing his eyes. Broad shoulders were proportionate to his thick biceps, straining against the sleeves of the polo shirt he had on. It was tucked into cargo pants, and she could see he was all muscle as he moved toward her.

Melissa blew out an irritated breath and stood, striding across the front porch. She didn't miss the way his gaze swept appreciatively up her body. Or the hint of a smile tugging on the corner of his mouth.

Typical.

Guys like him probably thought women would fall at their feet everywhere they went.

Heck, maybe they did.

But she'd done that song and dance already. She sure the hell never planned to date a man in uniform again. He could be the hottest Marine ever to walk the face of the Earth and she wouldn't give him a second look.

Besides, with her long red hair and feminine curves, she was used to men staring at her. Watching as she walked past. Hinting that they'd love to take her out.

She primly held out her hand in greeting as Tyler jogged up the steps to the front porch, and suddenly his muscular hand was clasping around hers, holding it just a beat too long.

"You're late."

His eyebrows raised as he pulled off his aviators. "Apologies, ma'am," he said, his striking green eyes sweeping over her with interest. "I couldn't get my date to leave."

"You had a date at ten on a Saturday morning?" she asked in disbelief.

"No. She was still here from last night," he added with a smirk.

"Well, isn't that lovely," she said, turning and walking back across the porch. She could feel his eyes on her ass as she walked, and she resisted the urge to swing her hips. Like she needed his type as a client.

Good grief.

"I would've appreciated some notice," she said. "I was about ready to leave. I've got back-to-back clients scheduled today."

He chuckled. "Jason said you were a handful."

She glanced over her shoulder to glare at him. "I'm doing Amy a favor by showing you this house. Normally we need financials, preapproval from your lender—the whole nine yards. We sit down and go over everything in the office. And normally my clients are courteous enough to arrive on time, not spend the morning in bed with their one-night-stand."

She fiddled with the lockbox as he came to a stop

behind her, and she tried to ignore his clean, masculine scent. Or the feel of his large frame hovering behind her. She could feel the heat radiating off his body, despite the slight chill in the air, and realized she liked it a little too much.

Which was ridiculous. So he'd showered and put on some aftershave before he came over. Big deal. He clearly didn't have an ounce of common courtesy.

And he was already seeing someone.

What type of woman he spent the night with, she didn't even want to know. Tyler had said his "date" wouldn't leave, but he didn't exactly seem like the dating type. More than likely, he'd picked up a woman at one of the bars in town and brought her home. Then tried to rush her out the door this morning.

Typical man.

She slid the key into the lock a moment later, and then she was pushing open the front door. Striding across the sleek wooden floors, her stilettos clicking with every step.

Tyler paused in the entryway, watching her as she glanced back at him. His broad shoulders filled the doorframe, and she forced herself to keep her eyes on his. "You're supposed to be looking at the house, not me."

He chuckled and gazed around. "Gorgeous."

She bristled slightly, wondering if he was referring to her or the home. Not that it mattered. He'd already pointed out that he'd been late because he was having sex with someone. Good grief. "It's three bedrooms, two and half baths," she began, running through her usual spiel. "Move-in ready, as you can see. On a third of an acre. The owners were military also and just moved out. It's going on the market first thing

Monday morning."

"Why are you waiting until then?"

"I'm having professional photos taken tomorrow, and then it will be listed."

Tyler strode across the empty living room, pausing in the door to the kitchen. "It might be more space than I need as a single guy, but it's a good investment. There's enough transition in the area with military and contractors coming and going all the time. I don't imagine I'd have trouble selling it in the future."

"Absolutely. Houses around here move quickly, as you know. The entire DC area market is hot right now. If you see something you're interested in, it won't be available for long."

He smirked. "Same with women. If I see someone I want, I go for it."

Melissa resisted the urge to roll her eyes. Was he really coming on to her? After admitting he'd been with a woman last night?

"That's lovely," she said, pasting a fake smile on her face. "Would you like to see the rest of the house?"

"Absolutely. Ladies first," he said, gesturing toward the stairs. The deep rumble of his voice sent a thrill shooting straight through her.

Ridiculous.

All his silly little innuendos were just to get under her skin.

She turned and walked ahead of him, tossing her long red hair over her shoulders. Determined not to let him rattle her. Goodness. Amy and Jason owed her big time after this. She hadn't expected the friend of Jason's from base to be more obnoxious than her ex.

And Michael had never acted like that when they were together. It was only after he called off the wedding that he'd turned into a total jackass.

"You seem rather different than Amy," Tyler commented. "She's a preschool teacher who loves running, and you're—"

"What?" Melissa asked breezily. "Out of your league?"

He chuckled. "Prancing around in stilettos. Wearing short skirts to show homes."

She smoothed her snug skirt absentmindedly as she took another step. It was snug, meant to accentuate her curves, but short? Not exactly. Her stiletto heel caught on the carpet just then, and she wobbled slightly, clutching onto the railing. Tyler's large hands landed on her hips, his broad chest at her back, and she resisted the urge to gasp.

Briefly, images of his muscular body moving behind her flashed through her mind. Positioning her how he wanted. Claiming her as his own as he whispered naughty fantasies into her ear.

Which was absurd.

Stiffening as she regained her footing, she cleared her throat. Took a purposeful step away from Tyler. "Amy teaches preschoolers," she said as she reached the landing. "I don't think suits and stilettos go with finger paint and playdough, do you?"

"Not exactly. I just expected someone more like her. Although Jason did warn me about you, don't get me wrong. I guess I should've taken his word for it," he added with a laugh.

"And pray tell, what did Jason say?" she asked. She tilted her head to gaze up at him, seeing the glimmer of amusement in his green eyes. Even with her sky-high heels, he still towered above her. She was right in line with his broad shoulders. He was entirely man and muscle—a force to be reckoned with. Cocky with the goods to back it up.

And she'd nearly fallen over on the stairs right in front of him, for heaven's sakes.

It wasn't like her to let a man rattle her so. Especially a client.

"I believe ball buster were the words he used," he said, those full lips quirking into a smile as he gazed down at her "I nearly fell off the barstool laughing."

"Why, did you have a few too many? You look like you should be able to hold your liquor."

His deep laughter filled the empty house. "Do I look like the kind of man who follows a woman around, dick in hand? I told him not to worry, I could handle anything you throw my way. As a matter of fact, I think we can work together just fine."

"Shall we move into the bedroom?" she asked innocently, turning and leaving him standing there at the top of the stairs.

Chapter 2

Tyler muttered a curse and strode across the upstairs landing to the master bedroom where Melissa had disappeared into. Of course his realtor would rival some sort of goddess. Flowing long red hair. Luscious curves. Full pink lips that he wouldn't mind devouring.

That sexy little suit she had on showed off her gorgeous body to its full advantage—supple breasts. Curvy hips. A shapely ass that he wouldn't mind digging his fingers into as she rode him straight to ecstasy. As he claimed her as his.

And hell.

He'd just left the woman he'd met last night. Given her a quickie this morning before he sent her on her way.

She didn't hold a candle to Melissa though.

And nights of meaningless sex were just that—meaningless. The woman he'd met at the bar last night had come home with him the second he'd asked. Fawned over him the entire night.

Melissa was a challenge he'd be eager to take. A beautiful woman he'd long to claim. If only she weren't his realtor.

Her eyes met his as he sauntered into the empty master bedroom. She gestured toward the bathroom on the left. "Full bath, dual vanities—for all your one-night-stands, I suppose."

He shook his head, amused, as she continued. "Large shower and whirlpool tub."

"For all my threesomes?"

She paused, looking momentarily taken aback.

"I'm just kidding, beautiful," he said in a low voice. "I love women, but I prefer one at a time."

Regaining her composure, she crossed the room, her shapely legs in stilettos doing wicked things to his libido.

"There's a great view," she continued, pulling back the curtains. "A fenced-in backyard. Mature trees."

He forced himself to lift his gaze from her ass. To look out the windows.

Hell.

He crossed his arms and looked around as she continued prattling off other features. Pretended to have an inkling of interest in the house. All thoughts of considering the purchase had temporarily gone out the window as soon as he'd seen her impatiently tapping her stiletto on the front porch.

Which was damn stupid.

He was ready to buy a house. The owners were moving back into his rental. He was ready for a place to call his own. And thinking with his dick wasn't going to help him out of his housing situation, no matter how tempting Melissa may be. There were other women out there.

Other redheads, even.

But would they all have that smart mouth and knowing gleam in their eyes?

"Let's continue," she said, walking toward the bedroom door. "I've got additional showings this afternoon."

"Are there other comparable homes on the market?" he asked, reluctantly following behind her.

Melissa nodded. "Absolutely. I expect this to move quickly though once the listing is live."

"Understood. Let's go see the rest of the house."

They walked through the other rooms and descended the stairs back into the foyer. "This is the first house I've looked at."

"It's understandable that you'd want to see more. Unfortunately, I do have other clients this afternoon. I could pull some specs tonight and see what else might be to your liking."

"Tomorrow?"

She nodded, her red hair swishing around her. "I could meet with you then. I'll need a firmer idea of price range though so I can determine the possibilities. And as I already mentioned, preapproval from your lender." She pulled her phone from her purse, scanning her calendar. "I'm meeting the photographer back here in the morning, but I have availability tomorrow afternoon."

Tyler scrubbed his hand over his jaw.

The smart thing to do would be to find a new realtor. To focus on finding a house to purchase, not the beautiful feminine curves of Melissa.

There was a part of him that couldn't resist her though. And hell if he didn't like the idea of seeing her again so soon. "I'll get everything to you this afternoon. And I do appreciate you meeting me here on such short notice. Jason knows my situation—I wasn't expecting to have to move so soon. I had a short-term lease, but I was expecting to be able to stay for a year. That's the military for you—people have to go where Uncle Sam says."

Melissa bristled slightly, and he raised a brow. There was a story there, he was sure. The second he'd mentioned the military, her expression had instantly changed. Maybe she'd been burned in the past.

"I'll be in touch," she said, holding out her slender hand.

He took it in his grip, enjoying the feel of her smooth skin against his calloused fingertips a little too much. Would she be that soft and smooth all over? He loved how even in those come-fuck-me heels, she still only came up to his shoulder. He was dying to slowly peel off that suit, press her against the wall, and kiss her everywhere. Run his tongue over all her feminine curves, touch her swollen sex, driving her crazy, and sink into oblivion.

With her still wearing those stilettos.

Redheads were always wild in bed, and he didn't doubt she would be either.

Not with that sassy mouth and those killer curves she seemed to enjoy flaunting.

Fucking her up against the wall wasn't exactly about to happen though. Not now and not ever.

She crossed the room, gathering her things. "I'll get the listing to you as well once it goes live. Unless of course you decide to put in an offer on this or something we see tomorrow. You can go on ahead," she said, nodding toward the front door. "I just need to send an email to my photographer while I'm thinking of it."

"I'll wait," he said in a low voice. "It's not safe for a woman to be alone in an empty house like this."

Melissa burst into laughter. "I didn't take you for such a gentleman."

"I'm not. Usually. But there's a 'Coming Soon' sign outside. A beautiful woman inside."

She tossed her red hair back over her shoulder. "I assure you that neither of us will be coming anytime soon."

He chuckled, his deep laughter filling the empty house. She was a firecracker. He crossed his arms, leaning against the counter. "Now who's the one with their mind in the gutter?"

"Just following your lead," she said innocently. She pulled an iPad from her bag and began to type up a quick email.

He watched her working for a moment, something stirring in his gut. Tyler cleared his throat. "Not to frighten you, but there was an attempted abduction of a woman showing houses a few counties over. We got an alert about it on base. Fortunately, she was able to get away, but the police put out a BOLO."

Melissa glanced up, her brows crinkling in confusion.

"Be on the lookout," he clarified. "I happened to see it because my buddy is one of the military police on base."

Melissa nodded, her focus back on the screen. She pressed a button to send her email. "Right, I did hear about that. I carry pepper spray with me. And usually I have a client's driver's license, etc. on file. This was kind of unusual agreeing to meet you like this."

"There's no guarantee as to who will show up at an open house though."

"There's not," she agreed, slipping her iPad back into the bag and gathering her things. "So, send me your information, and we'll talk."

She walked back across the room toward the foyer, her stilettos clicking on the hardwood floor. He tried to ignore the slight sway of her hips. The way her skirt cling to her ass. For the briefest flash, Tyler had a vision of her walking toward him like that, in a home of their own.

Sauntering in after a full day of work.

Pulling him toward her for a searing kiss and evening of sin.

Which was ridiculous.

He didn't seriously date, and he sure as hell never intended to live with a woman. Maybe in ten years or something when he was finally ready to settle down.

But at the moment?

Playing the field worked just fine for him. Bringing a woman home for the night and then never seeing her again.

And as for Melissa?

He had a feeling she'd be on his mind the rest of the day.

Chapter 3

Melissa strode into the bar that night, the silk blouse she had tucked into her skinny jeans clinging to her like a second skin. The pale lavender shade made her red hair stand out even more, and not a few guys sitting near the front of the restaurant gave her appreciative looks as she walked past. She'd curled her red hair so it cascaded around her shoulders, and a long silver pendant hung between her breasts, bouncing slightly as she walked.

Her best friend Amy always had said she had curves to die for—and although it was hell finding clothes to fit sometimes, when she had an outfit she looked good in, she loved to flaunt her assets.

She moved through a group of guys, feeling sexy and seductive in her stilettos. Maybe she wasn't planning on going home with anyone tonight, but she certainly didn't mind the attention.

She spotted Amy and Jason sitting at the bar, frowning as she realized that they were with someone.

Meeting her best friend and her boyfriend for drinks didn't mean she wanted them to set her up. Especially not after Tyler had already rattled her nerves this morning.

Goodness.

She'd barely even dated since Michael called off their wedding. There had been a short fling with a guy she'd met at the gym, but that barely counted since he was rebound all the way. And they'd spent most of their time between the sheets, no words needed.

But *dated* dated?

As in went out with a guy, actually got to know him before sleeping with him?

Hadn't happened.

And her one fling since Michael didn't actually count as moving on, did it?

It sure didn't feel like she'd moved on from the way he'd trampled on her heart.

The third person in their party took a swig of his beer, the sight of his sleeve bunching over his bicep doing funny things to her insides. Her stomach fluttered as she walked closer, taking in his broad shoulders and muscular arms, and then he was glancing at her walking toward them, a grin on his face.

Melissa resisted the urge to do a double take at Tyler eyeing her appreciatively. Tried to ignore the butterflies suddenly fluttering inside her stomach. She smiled at her best friend and waved, sliding onto the empty barstool between her and Tyler. She set her sequined clutch down on the bar, her newly manicured nails gleaming in the overhead lights. "Couldn't wait until tomorrow to see me?" she asked Tyler, pursing her freshly glossed lips.

He chuckled, the low sound making heat coil down from her abdomen. Causing her pussy to clench. The snug shirt Tyler had on stretched across his impressive chest, showing off his muscled physique. Those broad shoulders were a sight to behold, and briefly she imagined him hovering over her. Pinning her arms on the bed as he held her in place. Bucked into her.

Spread her legs wide and took her. Claiming her as his.

Making her scream his name.

"What makes you think I'm here to see you, beautiful?"

"Hey hun!" Amy said, giving her a one-armed hug around her shoulders. "I hope you don't mind that Tyler wanted to join us. Jason mentioned that we were meeting you here, and he decided to come, too."

"Mind? Why would I mind?" she asked, gesturing to the bartender. "I barely got a chance to listen to his witty banter this morning."

Jason laughed from the other side of Amy, glancing over at Melissa with his piercing blue eyes. Small crinkles formed in the corners, and his large hand came to a rest on the back of Amy's neck, lightly caressing her. It was simple yet intimate, and Melissa blinked. Tried to push away the feelings rising within her.

Things had been like that with Michael, too.

They'd set the date. Selected a wedding cake. Invited two hundred of their closest family and friends.

And then he'd bluntly told her he didn't want to marry her.

Acted like cancelling the wedding and the rest of

their life together meant nothing.

Just a blip on the radar.

"I hope Tyler didn't give you too much of a hard time this morning," Jason said, drawing her mind back to the present. "I told him you could take whatever he dishes out."

"Not at all," Melissa said smoothly, adjusting the sleek pendant that hung between her breasts. She felt Tyler's heated gaze on her but didn't look in his direction. "I showed him the house, and he managed to mention his one-night-stand only a handful of times. Did you know he was late meeting me because he couldn't get her to leave?"

The bartender walked over to take her order, laying a clean towel he'd been drying glasses with down on the bar. "What can I get you?"

"Dirty martini."

"Rookie move, man," Jason said with a chuckle as the bartender walked away.

Tyler leaned forward on the bar, his green eyes pinning Melissa in place. It was crazy how every time he looked at her it felt like he could see right through her. He didn't know the first thing about her, and he certainly never would. Not in anything other than a professional manner, if they were to work together.

She watched him, her lips parting slightly in surprise.

His gaze lowered to her mouth, pausing there a moment, and then he met her eyes again. "Did you get those papers I emailed you earlier?" Tyler asked, his voice low.

"I did," she said, turning toward him. "Although if you were planning to join us tonight, you could've just brought them here."

"And miss the look of surprise on your face when you saw me? Not a chance," he said, taking a pull from his longneck. Melissa watched his Adam's apple bob, taking in the whiskers on his chiseled jaw. Although he'd been freshly shaved this morning, a five o'clock shadow had already formed, albeit somewhat faint with his blond hair.

He smelled slightly of cologne, something clean with a hint of spice, and she wondered if he'd put some on before coming.

If he came out with his friend Jason tonight only because he knew that she'd be here.

"Like what you see?" he asked, his full lips quirking in a smile. God, he was seriously too much. Not to mention too handsome for his own good.

"What happened to your date from last night?" she asked sweetly. "Did she get bored of you already?"

"Like I told you this morning—I had to ask her to leave."

"So you only do one-night-stands?"

"Beautiful, I'll do any woman who wants me," he said in a low voice.

"How lovely."

"So, what'd you think of the house?" Amy asked, interrupting them. "Melissa said it's not even on the market yet. The homes have been moving so quickly, it's great you were able to get a look before it's even been listed."

"Like I told Melissa earlier, gorgeous."

She turned toward Amy and rolled her eyes as Amy cast her a knowing glance. Her long brown hair was pulled back in a ponytail, and she looked happy beside Jason. Although they lived across the street from one another, they'd only recently begun dating. Melissa was thrilled to see her best friend so happy, but it had brought about changes in her own life. Among their foursome of friends, she was the only single one.

And she was supposed to be planning her wedding, she thought with disdain. Not picking up the pieces of her life and moving on.

The bartender brought over her drink, and she took a sip of her martini.

"Jason and I are going away for the long weekend," Amy said.

"Where to?" Tyler asked, glancing over at his buddy. He was so tall he could gaze right over Melissa and Amy.

Hmmph. Everyone at the bar probably thought they were two couples sitting together. Not that Tyler was her type. At all.

"Skiing at Wintergreen."

"I didn't know you skied," Melissa said, flipping her hair over her shoulder. She felt Tyler's gaze on her again but kept her focus on Jason and Amy.

"Not nearly as much as Amy does," Jason admitted. "She'll probably be putting me to shame on the slopes. Maybe I can find some third grader to ski with me," he joked. "That's probably more my pace."

"Oh come on, I'll slow down for you," Amy teased. "Besides, it's payback for how fast he runs. Jason says he's slowing his pace so I can keep up, but I doubt it sometimes. Considering that I run several times a week, he's faster than I can ever hope to be."

"Oh God," Melissa groaned. "All of that sounds like too much work—running, skiing. What's next? Date night at the gym?"

"So I take it you don't ski?" Tyler asked.

"I sunbathe," Melissa said.

He smirked. "In the middle of winter?"

"My ideal destination for winter would be a tropical getaway—no need to escape the cold for more cold. Skiing sounds…awful."

"But you don't have any vacations planned?"

She stiffened slightly. She and Michael had cancelled their honeymoon trip to Bora Bora when the wedding had been called off. In a few short weeks, she should've been walking down the aisle. Marrying the guy she thought was the man of her dreams. Jetting off on the tropical vacation of a lifetime—soft sand, warm sun, and a honeymoon dreams were made of.

Not that she wanted a man who clearly no longer wanted her.

Still, she didn't need a reminder of a trip that wasn't to be. "Not unless I want the honeymoon suite to myself," she said sarcastically.

Tyler's gaze narrowed. "You're engaged?" His eyes slid to her empty ring finger.

She held up her hand, waggling her fingers. "Not anymore. Maybe I should thank him for saving me a lifetime of regret." Her phone began to buzz in her purse, but she ignored it for the moment, her gaze firmly set on Tyler. "My asshole of an ex called off the wedding. Better sooner rather than later, I suppose. If he'd left me standing at the altar, you'd be reading his obituary."

"His loss," Tyler said, his gaze softening slightly.

Melissa shrugged, taking a sip of her martini. "He was deployed a lot. I guess it's natural for some couples to grow apart given the circumstances. Still, a head's up would've been nice. A little warning, perhaps. He was getting cold feet while I was planning our wedding. Then we had to cancel every last thing."

"He's military?"

"Stationed at Quantico. Maybe you know each other. He's the asshole with a huge ego and tiny dick."

Tyler sputtered on his beer as Melissa raised her martini. "Onward and upward," she declared. "Michael didn't know what he was missing."

"Absolutely his loss," Amy said, clinking her beer bottle against Melissa's glass.

"Hear hear," Jason agreed. "You're better off without that guy. Any man who couldn't see what he was missing obviously wasn't the right one for you."

"Damn straight," Melissa said.

Her phone began buzzing again, and she frowned. She pulled it from her clutch and saw two missed calls from her sister.

"Is everything okay?" Amy asked, catching the expression on her face.

"I don't know," she said, swiping the screen to call her back. "Becky just called me twice. She's out in California, so it's a few hours earlier than here, but still. It seems unusual on a Saturday evening."

"I hope she's all right," Amy murmured.

Melissa rose from the barstool, doubt beginning to creep in. Tyler reached out to assist her, a brief flash of concern flickering in his green eyes. She let go of his muscular hand, grabbing her clutch from the bar and striding away.

She felt his gaze on her from behind but kept going, walking through the crowded bar area and edging around the packed tables. She and her sister usually chatted on Sunday evenings. If Becky was calling her several times on a Saturday night, something must be up. She pushed open the door to the patio, the cool night air biting into her. There were heat lamps outside and an awning stretched over the top along with temporary plastic walls, but none of it was a match for the cold.

The somewhat mild afternoon had given way to typical winter weather.

She shivered slightly, a frown on her face as the door shut behind her.

Her silky top wasn't enough to keep her warm out here. And she'd ridiculously come to the bar without a coat, not wanting to carry it around all night. The phone rang a couple of times as Melissa's gaze tracked over the couples outside, and then Becky finally answered, hysterical.

"He's missing!" she shrieked.

"Who?" Melissa asked, glancing around at the happy revelers. Saturday night was going on as usual here, with couples laughing, people throwing back drinks, and music blaring over the speakers.

And over the phone line, her sister sounded like she was falling apart. Melissa's stomach clenched at her sister's sobs. "Becky? What happened? What are you talking about?"

"Brody's missing!"

"Missing, like, *missing* missing? Missing in action?"

"Yes!"

Melissa muttered under her breath, turning away from the patio crowd. This wasn't the place to try and calm her sister down. She could barely even hear herself think, let alone carry on a conversation.

Striding back into the restaurant, she nearly bumped into a guy headed out the door. He eyed her appreciatively but moved on toward his own friends.

Glancing over at the bar, she saw Amy, Jason, and Tyler sitting there, happily throwing back beers without a care in the world. And why should they be worried?

It was Saturday night.

It's not like they had a clue her sister's world could potentially be falling apart.

Walking back across the restaurant, Melissa pushed open the front door and headed across the crowded parking lot. She clicked the remote of her white SUV and climbed into the driver's seat, shivering.

"Okay, tell me what's happening," she said as she started the engine, cranking up the heat. Cool air blasted from the vents, but it would warm up momentarily. She turned on her headlights, glancing around the busy lot.

"His Commanding Officer contacted me. Usually the MPs come when there's been a casualty, but since Brody is missing, there was nothing like that. No one showed up at my door or anything, but his CO called me."

She choked on a cry, and Melissa released a breath she hadn't even realized she'd been holding. "So that's good, right?" she said, a million thoughts racing through her mind. "I think Michael told me the MPs and a chaplain would come in case of a casualty. It doesn't matter the time of day or night, they'd show up at your door. This was kind of just a head's up, right? Like something might be wrong, but he's probably okay. They just wanted to update you and make sure you know what's happening."

Her sister whimpered on the other end of the line. "I have a bad feeling. Something's just not right. Brody's been deployed four times. I've never gotten a call like this before. Never."

"Well of course you're worried," Melissa soothed, heat finally coming through the vents of her SUV. She relaxed slightly into her seat. "I would be, too. But missing? I mean, what happened? Was he injured or something like that? Could they even tell you any details?"

"Nope. Operational security and what not. I don't know if his whole team's gone or just Brody or what."

"Bastards," Melissa spat out.

Her sister sniffled through her laughter. "I understand, I suppose. I mean what if someone else had been injured? I wouldn't want Brody in harm's way just because their spouse or significant other demanded to immediately know exactly what happened."

"So when will they update you?"

"I don't know. His CO just called me a little while ago. Honestly, it was the last call I expected. I mean, if I saw MPs pull up in my driveway, I would've lost my shit. But this? It wasn't even on my radar. I was going ready to go out and meet some friends for dinner later on. Then I get this call that could potentially change my entire life."

"Do you want me to fly out there?" Melissa asked. "I can catch a redeye out of Dulles or Reagan National. I'm sure I could find something, even last minute."

"No, no, don't come out here yet. I'll be fine. I just panicked you know? I'll be with my friends tonight, and they can wait with me for updates. And you're right, he's probably fine and I'm just blowing this way out of proportion."

"Right," Melissa said. "He's a strong guy. He has to be fine. Maybe there was some kind of fire fight and he's just hunkered down somewhere. And I haven't heard anything on the news about it, so it's probably a minor thing. I mean, if several Marines were injured or killed, it'd be on the news right?"

Becky blew out a sigh. "I guess. Maybe. Where are you anyway? I could barely hear you when I first called."

"The bar in town. I met up with Amy and Jason for drinks tonight. I'm in the car now though. It was so loud in there."

"God. Brody was supposed to be getting out of the military soon. How could he be fine for years and have this happen now?"

"He probably is fine," Melissa soothed. "They probably just want you in the loop. I mean God knows, when Michael and I were together, I would've wanted an update on him. Even if it turned out to be nothing, I'd want to know as soon as possible."

"Yeah, you're right. Go back to your friends. I didn't mean to totally ruin your Saturday night."

"You did not ruin my Saturday night. And you know you can call me anytime."

"I know, I know. I'll call you if I hear anything else. I think I just needed to talk myself down off the ledge. I mean, he's fine, right? He has to be."

"Exactly," Melissa agreed. "Of course he's fine."

The two said their goodbyes, and Melissa tucked her phone back into her sequined clutch. Goodness. If that didn't kill her mood to drink with her friends. Her sister was all the way on the other side of the country scared out of her mind. Worried that her own fiancé would never make it home from Afghanistan to her. It was bad enough that Melissa's relationship had ended so badly, but Becky and Brody were madly in love. Pretty much the perfect couple.

She climbed out of her SUV and hurried back across the parking lot, her heart pounding in her chest. It felt like she'd just dodged a bullet or something, and they didn't even know how Brody was. If he was okay.

Amazing how one little phone call could completely rattle you. The news from Becky had sent a shock straight through her system.

She no longer felt like hanging out with Amy and Jason or dealing with Tyler's cocky attitude. She had work to do for tomorrow. Confirming the list of photos she'd need of the house. Listings to go through for her other clients. Potential houses for Tyler.

Goodness, she had her own sister to worry about. Her sister's fiancé.

She'd tell Amy she was leaving and just call it a night.

Pulling open the door to the bar and striding back in, Melissa did a double take as Tyler was suddenly right at her side. Even in her stilettos he still towered above her, but instead of feeling relief or excited nervousness at seeing him, she just felt sad. Defeated.

His green eyes locked with hers. "I went out on the patio to see if you were okay, beautiful. Amy was worried when you didn't come back."

"My sister called."

"And?" He cocked an eyebrow. The dark leather jacket he had on made it seem like he was ready to leave himself. He didn't appear at all rushed though—just completely and totally focused on her.

Melissa's voice wavered slightly as she tried to speak, and she cleared her throat. Swallowed. "Her fiancé is missing."

"Missing?"

"He's deployed to the Middle East. She's out in California finishing school. His commanding officer contacted her to say that Brody was missing in action."

"Shit," Tyler muttered.

Melissa unwittingly took a step back. "That's bad, right? I told her it was okay since the MPs didn't show up, but people just don't go missing in Afghanistan. Not unless it's something serious. Oh my God, what if he was killed? Missing means they can't find the body!"

Tears smarted her eyes, and Tyler took a step closer to her, his hand landing on her forearm. His touch soothed her, grounding her amidst the turmoil racing through her. Anchoring her in place.

The warmth from his touch burned through her silky blouse, sending awareness through her entire body. The heat from his large frame radiated off him. Her eyes met his.

"It doesn't mean anything other than what it means," he said in a low voice. "It means we wait for news. Hope like hell for the best."

She sniffled, raising a trembling hand to wipe away a stray tear.

His jaw clenched as he gazed down at her. "Hell, don't cry, beautiful."

"But she's my sister—and he's gone. They're engaged, and he's just—missing. Just like that."

Without another word, he pulled her into his muscular embrace. She sniffled against him, finally relaxing into his touch. Inhaling his scent. He was solid and strong—a rock in the midst of chaos. The soft cotton of his shirt felt smooth and comforting beneath her cheek. The scent of his leather jacket enveloped her, mixed in with the spice of his aftershave.

She felt safe for a brief moment—secure.

Odd that she'd feel that way about Tyler—a man of one-night-stands and the arrogant attitude that just didn't quit.

He was a Marine though, just like Brody. He knew what it meant to lose someone.

She shivered slightly against him, hoping against hope that Brody was okay, and Tyler tightened his arms around her.

A moment later, she heard Amy and Jason beside her, her best friend asking what was wrong. Melissa pulled back from Tyler and relayed what she'd just learned from Becky. Amy's hands rose to her face as she gasped, and Jason frowned, looking worried.

"Are you flying out there?" Amy asked.

"She said not to right now. I guess I'll wait and see what happens—I'll go if she needs me. I mean maybe it's nothing. Maybe he's all right and it's just some sort of miscommunication and we'll hear from them soon."

"Right, he could be totally fine," Amy said. Jason and Tyler exchanged a glance.

"Maybe he'll be okay," Melissa insisted. "They don't know anything really. Not yet."

"She doesn't want you to wait with her?" Amy asked. "I mean, just in case…."

"I think she didn't want me flying across the country tonight if it's unnecessary. Becky has her friends out in California. She'll be with them tonight. I mean, God, hopefully this is all just some big misunderstanding and he'll be fine. The second she wants me there, though, I'll be on the next plane. If she doesn't need me right now, I'll wait."

Amy gave her a quick hug. "Let me know if you need anything. If Becky needs something. I know there's not much we can do, but sitting around waiting and wondering and assuming the worst has got to be awful."

"Maybe I'll try to convince her to come here—she's got classes though," Melissa added, thinking out loud. "She probably won't want to drop everything and come. Not unless she has to, of course."

"I'll see what I can find out from my commander on base," Jason said. "Maybe I can get some updates that she wouldn't be able to."

Melissa nodded and thanked him. "I'd appreciate it. Becky would, too. I think she just immediately assumed the worst, so any information you can find out would be great."

"Of course," Jason said.

"Do you feel like getting a table? It's kind of loud in the bar area," Amy said. "Maybe something a little quieter would be better."

"I think I'm just going to call it a night. I'm not in the mood for drinks anymore."

Amy nodded sympathetically. "Are you sure you don't want something to eat?"

"No, I'm fine. I'll let you know if I find out anything else. And Tyler, I guess I'll see you tomorrow, assuming my sister doesn't need me to come out there."

"We can reschedule. I understand if you need to go stay with her."

"No, I'll pull the specs in the morning when I'm meeting with the photographer. I have to let him into the home to take the photos, but I can work while I wait. We can see a few houses in the afternoon."

He nodded. "All right. I'll walk you to your car."

"I'm right outside," she protested.

"Then it'll be a short walk," he quipped, wrapping his arm around her shoulder to guide her toward the door.

She gripped her clutch in one hand, allowing him to guide her out. "Oh, I never paid for my drink!" she said, suddenly stopping. "I should go back."

"I already got it," he said easily.

"What?"

"I paid for your drink, beautiful. When you were on a call with your sister. No need to thank me."

She frowned as she walked ahead of him outside, the slight breeze ruffling her hair. This entire night was starting to feel surreal. Her sister's fiancé was missing. Tyler was acting concerned about her after his cocky attitude earlier when they'd first met.

He'd insisted on walking her out.

What was next?

Maybe she'd stumble and break a heel, ruining her favorite pair of stilettos.

"Melissa," a male voice said, distracting her from her thoughts, and she spun to the left, halting in her tracks. Her heart pounded in her chest as her mouth dropped open in surprise. "I didn't expect to see you here," he said.

Chapter 4

Michael stood a few feet away, his brow crinkling in confusion as Tyler came to a stop beside her. He hadn't shaved in a couple days, and while she used to like the ruggedly sexy look on him, now he looked unappealing as hell.

Amazing how a man calling off your wedding could do that sort of thing to a girl.

A few months ago, she'd thought he was the best thing that had ever happened to her. A man no one else could live up to.

And now?

Just standing near him put a sour taste in her mouth.

Michael's gaze swept between her and Tyler, realization crossing his face. His gaze briefly trailed over her clingy blouse and full breasts. Tracked back up to meet her gaze. "I didn't realize you were seeing anyone."

Melissa stiffened, leaning ever-so-slightly into

Tyler.

How was she supposed to explain this? She didn't exactly want to tell her ex that he was just her client. That he was friends with Jason and Amy.

Tyler wrapped his arm her shoulder, pulling her close. "You must be the ex-fiancé," he said with a smirk. "I've heard all about you."

Michael frowned.

"Tyler Braxton," Tyler said, holding out a muscled hand.

Michael cleared his throat, finally gripping Tyler's hand and introducing himself.

"We were just headed out, right, beautiful?" Tyler said.

Melissa recovered, plastering a smile on her face. "That's right, snookums," she said sweetly as Tyler choked back a laugh. She slid her arm around his waist, nestling into his solid frame. "We should get going. I know you're tired after being up all last night. You're insatiable, aren't you?"

She glanced up at him and smiled, amusement twinkling in Tyler's eyes.

"Some people say that," he admitted.

"I should get going," Michael choked out.

"Absolutely," Tyler agreed. "I prefer having Melissa all to myself."

He smirked as Michael clenched his jaw, and then they were continuing on their way, Tyler seeming to know where she was parked. Melissa glanced back over her shoulder, watching her ex hurry away. He nearly bumped into a couple leaving the bar in his haste to get inside.

"How'd you know this was my car?" she asked Tyler.

"I saw it this morning. Did you forget you'd parked right in the driveway?"

Melissa blew out an exasperated sigh, pulling away from him. She instantly missed the warmth of his body, but that didn't mean they needed to stand here in the parking lot with their arms around each other.

They weren't dating or something.

They weren't anything.

"I didn't realize you had such a memory for detail. Thank you for walking me to my car," she said, her gaze darting back to the restaurant as the doors swung shut behind Michael.

Tyler raised a brow. "And you're welcome for rescuing you back there."

"Hmmph. I could've handled it myself."

"You could have," he agreed. "Maybe I have a thing for damsels in distress."

"Maybe I'm not in distress," she countered.

His full lips quirked. "Maybe not. Doesn't mean I minded holding you close. I'll see you tomorrow, beautiful. Drive safely."

Her mouth dropped open in surprise, and he chuckled. "I never imagined you as the type to be rendered speechless."

"I never imagined you as the type to have manners."

He chuckled, taking the keys from her. His fingers briefly caressed hers, and she startled at his touch. At the warmth of his skin brushing against hers. Tyler clicked the key fob and opened the door to her SUV, gently guiding her inside before handing the keys back over. "You're cold," he said in a low voice. "And it's been a long night."

She opened her mouth, but before she could even

utter a response, he was shutting the door. Turning away.

She locked the doors and then started the engine, watching in the rearview mirror as Tyler disappeared into the parking lot. He was a puzzle, that one. Shoot, knowing him, he was probably heading back into the bar for another beer and a new woman for the night. And not that she knew him.

He seemed to enjoy that silly little act they'd put on for Michael. Wrapping his arm around her shoulder and pulling her close. Never mind that their little performance was over the second it started.

She had enough to worry about without letting her ex get under her skin.

So what if he thought she'd moved on already. It served him right.

Pulling her phone from her clutch, she sent her sister a text.

Call me the moment you hear anything. Day or night. I'm headed home. Xoxo

Her phone buzzed almost immediately with Becky's reply.

I will. I just keep telling myself this is all a misunderstanding. That Brody is fine.

Melissa nodded to herself, thumbing a quick response.

Of course he's fine. He has to be.

Becky didn't respond immediately, and she sighed. Not knowing had to be worse than knowing the truth, didn't it?

***

Tyler sauntered across the parking lot, grumbling.

Since when did he help a woman into her car and then leave? That wasn't exactly his style. Ever. Normally he'd be taking a woman home from the bar, not sending her on her merry way. Hell, hadn't he done exactly that last night?

Jason and Amy were still inside, ordering dinner, but once Melissa had said she was leaving, he'd decided to call it a night, too.

And wasn't that unexpected.

Jason wouldn't have been surprised in the least if Tyler had gone back in and chatted up a woman. He just wasn't in the mood for a random hookup though. Not when the memory of Melissa in his arms was emblazoned in his brain.

Her soft curves pressed up against him.

Her silky red hair swishing around every time she moved.

Women like that were dangerous—used to attracting men wherever they went. If he wasn't careful, she'd have him eating right out of her hand.

Odd that he felt protective of her though. Despite the façade she put on for the world, he sensed there was something more vulnerable and fragile beneath. Maybe it was that her ex had called off their wedding. Maybe it was something else.

Not that he'd ever find out. He'd meet her tomorrow, hopefully find a home in the next week or so, and then move on with his life. Move in to his house, meet a new woman every week. Continue on as life had always been.

His phone buzzed in his pocket, and he pulled it out, answering in a low voice.

"Tyler, bro, we're all down at the pool hall," his friend Braden said. Tyler heard voices and the crack of the cue ball in the background, followed by a round of laughter. "I thought you were meeting us here."

Tyler muttered a curse. That had been the plan—until Jason had mentioned Melissa's name. He wouldn't normally hang out with his buddy and girlfriend, but when they'd mentioned her?

Game over.

He'd ditched his buddies just to see the look on her face when she'd shown up at the bar.

And hell it had been worth it.

Wide eyes. Full breasts bouncing as she moved. Those pink lips he couldn't get enough of. And that gorgeous red hair. "I swung by the bar for a drink. Met up with Jason and a couple of others. I'll be there in thirty."

Braden chuckled. "A drink, huh? We've got pitchers of beers here. I don't suppose she has a name?"

"Who?" Tyler asked as he climbed into his SUV.

"The woman you're not taking home with you tonight."

He chuckled. "I'm taking a night off," he said, starting the engine. He revved it a couple of times, feeling his SUV rumble beneath him. Hell if he wouldn't mind off-roading through some of the open space around here. Taking his baby out for a drive over the open land. On a gorgeous night like tonight, he could cut through the field and head down to the lake. Not that that sort of thing was fun alone.

But with a blanket and beautiful woman? A private night under the open sky was damn perfect. He couldn't exactly drag a woman he'd just met at the bar out there though.

It was too secluded for a woman to agree to go with a man she just met.

And he wasn't the type to have a serious girlfriend.

Maybe a group of them could head over one weekend. Bring a cooler of beers and some women and enjoy the night air. Briefly, Melissa flashed through his mind, but he brushed that thought aside. Even if she was friends with Jason and Amy, it didn't mean he'd be taking her along with him.

"Uh-huh," Braden said, drawing his mind back to the present. "More like you crashed and burned, which isn't your usual MO. Liam and Grayson are already here. We all know Jason never joins us. Get your ass over here."

"Yeah, yeah. Don't get your panties in a twist. I'm on my way."

Twenty minutes later he was pulling into the pool hall on the outskirts of town. The well-worn florescent sign hung above the front door, and paint was beginning to peel on the exterior of the building. A few guys stood around outside smoking, and he pulled into the lot, gravel crunching beneath his tires.

The bar they usually frequented was in the small town near Quantico—full of plenty of local women eager to meet a Marine. Although the pool hall had a rougher crowd, he and his buddies never ran into trouble.

No one was about to mess with a group of military men.

Pulling into a free space, he crossed the gravel lot, stuffing his keys into his front pocket.

Ironic how he'd just tucked Melissa into her fancy SUV and then headed over here. A woman like that was probably used to being wined and dined. Hadn't she said her honeymoon was supposed to be in fucking Bora Bora?

Not that he was exactly piss poor or something. He'd saved his hard-earned cash to make a down payment on a house. Had learned the value of a dollar from his working-class parents.

That didn't mean he and Melissa didn't come from different worlds though.

Maybe he was comfortable now, but that didn't mean he didn't know what it meant to do without. He had a feeling she'd been handed everything on a silver platter her entire life. Maybe she worked hard as a realtor now, but he was willing to bet mommy and daddy had helped pay for her college education.

He'd joined the Marines at eighteen to make something of himself. Just like most of the other guys he knew.

Pulling open the door to the pool hall, he strode inside. Low music thumped over the speakers, conversations carried on around him, and he heard some of the waitresses giggling as a few patrons tried to chat them up. He paid for a couple of rounds of pool and headed off to the back where his buddies were.

They liked the corner table to see what was going on around them. That and years of training in the military had made them constantly aware of their surroundings. They could easily see who was coming and going from there.

Not that he expected to run into trouble.

Sauntering across the room, Braden looked up and chuckled. "About time you showed up," he said with a grin.

"You fellas missed me?" Tyler said with a smirk.

"Or you couldn't meet any women without me around." He shrugged out of his leather jacket and grabbed an empty pilsner glass, pouring himself a beer from the full pitcher. An empty one already sat to the side.

"In your dreams, pretty boy," Braden said. "Liam's been flirting with the waitresses all night long. Grayson and I need someone who's actually ready to play pool."

"Hey now," Liam said with a laugh, running his hand through his cropped blond hair. His blue eyes glinted with amusement. "How many times have we watched you chase tail, bro?"

"Hoorah," Grayson said, sauntering up to them. "So, who's the babe?" he asked Tyler. "You're late because you were grabbing drinks with a woman?"

"There's no babe," he said, a wave of protectiveness washing over him. So what if he did find Melissa hot as hell? He didn't want his buddies imagining what she looked like. He didn't want them thinking of her at all.

"I guess not since you're here with us. What happened to the woman from last night?" Grayson asked. "She get bored of you already?"

"Too clingy. I could hardly get her to leave this morning."

"Shit, next time go to her place," Braden said with a chuckle. "Disappear in the middle of the night like any self-respecting Marine."

"Well that's classy as fuck," Tyler said. "I don't always stay the night, but I do give them a parting gift before I go on my merry way."

"A parting gift," Braden snorted.

Tyler leaned back against the pool table, taking a

swig of the hoppy brew. "A couple of orgasms never hurt anyone. Leaves them wanting more."

"So that's why your name and number's plastered all over the ladies' room," Liam quipped.

"And you would know, asshole," Tyler said.

"And yet you still went for drinks with a woman and didn't take her home? Most be true love," Grayson countered, grabbing his cue.

"Hell, she's my realtor," Tyler said, walking over to pick up his own. He set his glass down on the table. "I need a house, not a beautiful woman for the night."

"What's the rush?" Liam asked, walking back over to them. "You've got a decent apartment."

"I've gotta move out of my apartment. They're converting them to condos or some shit like that."

"So buy that," Braden said. "Problem solved."

"I'm ready to have a place of my own. I could just do another rental, but I've had it with landlords and small one-bedrooms."

"Think you'll stick around Virginia long enough to make buying a house worth it?" Braden asked, raising his eyebrows. "I'm only here two years before my next assignment."

"That's the plan. I've been deployed damn near enough times. After this stint at Quantico is over, I'll be leaving active duty. Maybe working at the Pentagon. I hate to say it, but a desk job is sounding pretty good right now."

Grayson shook his head, racking the balls. "I can't see it, man. You, at a nine-to-five desk job? No fucking way."

Tyler shrugged. "What the hell are we doing on base now?"

"Temporary duty. Training the young 'uns."

Tyler smirked. "Hell, if you want to get deployed again, go for it. I'm just saying I've had my fill. When my last two years are up, I'm out."

Braden walked over, taking a swig of his beer. "All right, boys, enough chit chat. Let's play some pool."

Chapter 5

The buzzing of Melissa's alarm clock woke her out of a restless sleep the next morning, and she fumbled with it, trying to turn off the blaring sound. Smacking it again and accidentally knocking the entire clock to the floor, she finally climbed out of bed and retrieved it, setting it back on the nightstand.

She stretched in her satin chemise, the lace bodice tugging across her full breasts.

It was a pity Michael never got to see all the sexy new lingerie she'd gotten at her bridal shower—the shower held before he'd called off their wedding. Not that she'd want him to see her in it now, she thought, running her hands over the smooth material.

His loss.

It was a pity her ex had turned out to be a complete and utter asshole. A coward. Maybe he fought bravely for his country and all that, but a lifelong commitment to the woman he supposedly loved?

A marriage and life together?

Apparently, that was out of the question.

Literally the only thing worse would have been if he'd actually left her at the altar. Been too cowardly to let her know ahead of the big day.

But this?

Equally aggravating in her mind. She'd wasted three years with him—dealt with his deployments, the uncertainty of when he'd be back, of if he was safe.

And now? She slept in her sexy little negligees every night. Her best friends had insisted she keep all of the shower gifts, and it would be a crime to let them linger in the bottom of her lingerie drawer. She felt sexy and fierce in it, even if it was for her eyes only.

For the moment.

Briefly she imagined what a man like Tyler would think of it, and just as quickly, she brushed that thought aside.

The lace bodice wrapped around her full breasts, leaving nothing to the imagination, and the chemise was so short it barely covered her bottom. Although it would've been exciting to wear it in Bora Bora and see the hungry look in her ex's eyes, she'd settle for feeling like a vixen in it for now.

Someday Tyler's hands would drag all over that silky material, running his rough hands over her curves. Sliding it further up her legs, revealing her further to him.

Well not Tyler.

But another man. One who wasn't obnoxious about discussing the women he slept with and didn't flirt relentlessly with her, constantly dropping hints and sexual innuendo. She could handle him, certainly.

It didn't mean a man like him would end up any more committed than her ex.

Flipping her long red hair over her shoulder, she padded across the plush carpet of her bedroom, grabbing her phone from the charger. There were three texts from Becky, and she quickly swiped the screen, her eyes running over the messages.

No updates on Brody.

His commander is hoping they're hunkered down somewhere.

I'm going to bed. Talk to you tomorrow. xx

Melissa blew out a sigh of relief. Hunkered down? That had to be a good thing. They were just hiding from the enemy. Biding their time. Maybe they were injured or trapped and couldn't immediately get back to base.

But he'd be okay.

The commander wouldn't have given Becky false hope, would he?

There was a missed call from the real estate photographer that she was meeting at eleven this morning. She dialed into her voicemail, listening to the message. God, he was kind of annoying to work with. Sometimes it seemed like he called just to hear himself speak.

And she had work to do.

Her phone rang a moment later, and one of her best friend's names, Beth, flashed across the screen. "Amy just told me about your sister," she said as soon as Melissa answered. "Is everything okay? Are there any updates?"

Melissa sank back down onto her bed, staring at her hot pink toenail polish. "I don't know. We're just waiting to hear any news at this point. It sounds like the commander is hopeful they're just hunkered down somewhere, hiding, not actually missing."

"Wow, I'm sorry. But that sounds like it might be good news."

"Yeah, I hope so," Melissa said, flouncing back down on her pillows. She blew out a sigh. It had been months since she'd had a man in her bed—and she missed that. She was angry as hell at her ex, but she missed the feel of a man's arms around her. Of the weight of him atop her.

It was lonely as hell sleeping alone every night.

"Are you coming with us to brunch later?" Beth repeated, drawing her back to the present.

"I can't today, hun. I'm meeting with the photographer at eleven for my newest listing and then showing some houses this afternoon."

"Bummer. We're meeting Amy and Jason at ten."

"Yeah, I wish I could come. Brunch sounds infinitely preferable to my day."

"Bad clients?"

Melissa laughed. "Believe it or not, the photographer is more annoying than today's client. And that's saying a lot. I'm helping Jason's friend Tyler find a house."

"Another Marine?" Beth asked doubtfully.

Melissa laughed. "Don't worry, I told him all about my asshole of an ex."

"While you were showing him houses?" Beth asked in disbelief.

"No, over drinks last night," she said, her gaze falling on the boxes stacked in the corner of her bedroom. Michael had left a few of his things here, and he'd never gotten them back. They were collecting dust in the corner now, and she was ready to haul them to the curb.

To be done with him and his things forever.

"Wait, you had drinks? Like a date?"

"No, not a date," Melissa said, rolling her eyes. "I met Amy and Jason last night, and he happened to show up. Which reminds me…." She launched into the story of running into Michael in the parking lot.

"Only you," Beth said with a laugh. "Who else has a hot man come to their rescue when their ex is around? I swear that type of thing never happened to me."

"You have a fiancé!" Melissa said.

"Now," Beth corrected. "I mean in the past. If I run into an ex, I'm sweaty and gross from the gym or something."

"Well, I'd been upset about my sister," Melissa huffed. "I was leaving because I'd just gotten off the phone with her."

"Sorry, hun. Are you flying out to California to wait with her?"

"She didn't want me to," Melissa said. "I guess we're just hoping for the best at this point. It's too early on the west coast for me to call her right now."

"Listen, I need to get going if I'm going to make it to brunch in time."

"Me, too. I set my alarm—on a SUNDAY for God's sake—because I have so much work to do. Search the latest listings, meet the photographer, upload the photos, do a couple of showings this afternoon. My day is killer."

"Well, you usually get to sleep in Monday mornings when the rest of the working world is heading out the door."

"Touché. Oddly enough, most people prefer home

showings on weekends, not first thing on Monday morning. Gotta give the people what they want."

Beth laughed. "How good of you to make that sacrifice. Let me know if you hear anything about Becky, all right? And good luck with the showings today. We'll miss you at brunch."

"And I'll miss that Bloody Mary. Thanks, sweetie. I'll talk to you later."

Melissa set her phone on the nightstand after ending the call, reluctantly getting out of bed for the second time that morning. A long, hot shower was in order, followed by some super strong coffee.

Chapter 6

Tyler jogged down the road near his apartment, his breath fogging in the brisk air. The cold made him wish he'd bundled up more, and he pushed himself harder, tugging the hood of his sweatshirt tighter around him.

He sure hadn't felt the cold last night, walking Melissa out to her SUV. Maybe it had been an unseasonably warm evening, but hell. Just the mere sight of her sent him up in flames. His interest flared any time she was near, and his cock immediately stood up and took notice.

Which was inconvenient since he was trying to work with her, not take her to bed.

Not yet anyway.

But hell. Even if he didn't find a single home he was interested in, it would be worth it just to wind her up. To see her beautiful mouth drop open in surprise before she came up with another witty comeback. To see her gorgeous curves, those full breasts rising and falling. To let his eyes wander over the form-fitting clothes he longed to peel right off her.

And the kicker was he actually needed a new place.

Sure, he could probably crash with one of his buddies from base, but the bottom line was, he had to move out of his apartment. He'd be shit out of luck if he screwed his realtor and ended up temporarily without a place to live.

Then again, it might actually be worth it just to spend a night with her. To spend some time exploring her gorgeous curves, finding out what drove her wild.

Listening to his name on her lips as he made her come.

He'd slept in worse places while deployed than a friend's sofa. Being temporarily without a place just might be worth it to spend a night with her.

Not that Melissa had seemed tempted by him in the slightest.

The ex-fiancé of hers did present a bit of a challenge. Maybe she was over him to a certain extent, but she might not be ready to sleep with another man. Especially another Marine.

And wasn't that just his bad luck?

For a man that had no problem finding a beautiful woman to spend the night with, it figured that he was tempted by the one woman who wasn't interested in him.

Who he shouldn't have.

The forbidden fruit and all that.

His phone buzzed with a text, and he pulled it from his running belt as he jogged, glancing down at the screen. He raised his eyebrows as he saw Melissa's name.

In bed with another woman this morning?

Meet me at noon.

He chuffed out a laugh, shaking his head. If she really thought he was with a woman, why the hell was she texting him? Holding the phone to his mouth, so he could talk while running, he dictated a reply to Melissa.

I'm out running. Alone.
Did you miss me, beautiful?

His phone buzzed with her reply, and his lips quirked.

Who are you running from?
I assume you're trying to get away from yet another clingy woman.

He held his phone up again.

That's a negative, gorgeous.
All thoughts of other women have been gone since I met you.

Melissa texted him immediately.

I thought men like you only think with your dicks?

He nearly choked on his laughter.

Why are you thinking of my dick?

His phone buzzed with her reply.

I'm not sleeping with you.

He smirked and sent her another text.

Never say never.
I'll see you at noon. Same house as yesterday?

His phone buzzed with a response.

Same place. Don't be late again.

He slowed down his jog and spoke in a low voice into his phone.

I'll be there on time if you wear those come-fuck-me heels.

He waited a beat, surprised she didn't respond as quickly.

Asshole.

He chuckled and held up his phone one last time.

Just teasing you, beautiful.

But if you're ever interested, I wouldn't turn you down.

Tucking his phone back into his running belt, his body warmed as he began to pick up his pace, running harder. Hell, she was a firecracker. He wished he was with her right now, getting his heart rate pumping. Moving over her beautiful body as he pounded into her.

Not running down the street in the damn cold.

If Melissa was in his bed, he'd sure as hell have no reason to leave it. She was the stuff fantasies were made of—all gorgeous curves, smooth skin, and a smart mouth.

Hell. That mouth.

He wouldn't mind letting her suck him deep, letting those pink lips wrap around his cock.

And hell.

Now he was getting hard while running.

He'd think of training on base. And the damn desert he'd been deployed to. And moving boxes.

Anything and everything but her.

***

Tyler pulled up to the house he'd met Melissa at yesterday, climbing out of his vehicle. Although they had a few homes to visit this afternoon, she was running late with her meeting with the photographer and had asked him to come here.

She'd sent him the listings earlier, and he felt like an ass never having asked about her sister this morning when they were texting. He was so busy trying to rile her up, he'd totally neglected to check and see if there were any updates on the missing boyfriend.

This, after she'd left early last night because she was upset.

Thinking with his dick had never done him any good in the past, and it sure as hell wasn't winning him any favors now. She'd been shocked when he did text and ask about her sister. No news was supposedly good news at this point, so they waited.

And continued on with their plans for the day, without Melissa up and flying out to California.

Melissa's white SUV was parked in the driveway, and there was a sedan on the street in front of the house. Tyler shut the door of his own vehicle and strode up the driveway, his gaze sweeping the area.

His eyes fell on the "For Sale" sign in the front yard again. Hopefully Melissa had locked the front door. He didn't like that she was alone showing homes all the time. Hell, she'd been alone with him, and he'd seen firsthand how easy it would be for someone to harm her.

No one else around.

A big empty house.

No one to hear if she screamed.

He knew realtors showed homes all the time, but something about the idea of Melissa being alone all the time didn't sit right with him.

And wasn't that a gut check.

He barely even knew her. Didn't have a claim to her whatsoever. And hell, hadn't he spent the past twenty-four hours imagining what it would be like to take her to bed? How many other men had she worked with who had similar thoughts?

She was an attractive female.

Gorgeous.

She was successful in her career. Certainly, she must take some basic safety precautions when working. He'd have to ask her about that. Just to exercise caution.

He frowned as he saw movement in the bushes of the side yard. Ignoring the front porch he'd been aiming for, he rounded the side of the house, shocked to see a man standing there in the shadows. He approached the man silently, adrenaline surging through him. "Looking for something?" Tyler asked in a gruff voice.

The man jumped back, fumbling with the camera in his gloved hands, and Tyler clenched his jaw, his gaze narrowing. "What the hell are you doing?" he ground out. His gaze moved from the window back to the man.

"I was just photographing this house for a listing. I'm working with the realtor inside. It's going on the market tomorrow morning." Tyler's gaze tracked over him. He had a dark wool coat on, neatly pressed khakis, and boots. He looked to be around forty or so, slightly balding. The stubborn way he held himself made Tyler feel like he'd caught him doing something he shouldn't though.

"By hiding in the bushes?" Tyler asked, taking a step closer.

The man recovered from his initial surprise, smoothing out his jacket. "I'm just getting all the angles of the property. It's standard for buyers to want to see the property from all vantage points."

Tyler moved closer, frowning. He glanced in the window, and his chest tightened as he saw Melissa sitting at the kitchen counter on a barstool, typing at her laptop. Her long legs were crossed, her skirt hitting at mid-thigh, and he resisted the urge to groan as he saw she did indeed have on another pair of stilettos.

Jesus Christ.

This woman was going to be the death of him. He was rock hard every time she was near.

And this window had a perfect view of her sitting there, working. Had this guy been…watching her? Melissa had said she was meeting with the photographer though. It seemed like an odd spot to photograph the property.

"Let me see your camera," he demanded, holding out a hand. "I want to see the pictures."

"What? I'm not handing over my camera. Who are you?"

"A friend," Tyler said, crossing his arms as he looked down at the smaller man. Tyler was younger, stronger, and no doubt faster than him. He could easily wrestle the camera from the man's hands if he wanted.

Instead of looking intimidated, the guy looked smug as he glanced back toward the window again. "Of Melissa's? She didn't mention any friends coming by."

"We're looking at houses together this afternoon. She asked me to meet her here—not that it's any of your damn business."

"Ah, so you're a client," the man said with a chuckle. "A little over-protective, aren't we? Melissa and I have worked together for over a year. I assure you I know what I'm doing when it comes to photographing properties and homes. Ms. Ford trusts me implicitly."

Ms. Ford?

Who the hell was this asshole?

Tyler watched as Melissa looked up just then, no doubt hearing their voices outside. She pointedly glanced down at the time on her watch and then clasped her hands to her chest in mock surprise.

"What's she doing?" the photographer asked, looking chagrined that he was missing out on the inside joke.

"She texted me this morning and told me to be on time," Tyler said with a smirk. His voice was low. Dangerous. "I'm sure you know how Ms. Ford doesn't like to be kept waiting."

Suddenly looking flustered, the man took a step back. "How strange. I called her earlier and never heard back. Several times, in fact. I wonder if she didn't get my voicemails. I wanted to see if she wanted me to pick up coffee for her on my way over. It's no trouble, and I know she always wants a strong cup first thing in the morning."

He glanced back at Tyler, seeming pleased that he had this tiny bit of knowledge about Melissa.

Good God.

Who didn't want caffeine after a late night? And hell. Tyler knew how his friends and coworkers drank their coffee, too. It didn't mean he got a hard-on over it like this asshole.

This dude clearly had a thing for Melissa. The story about photographing the property from the bushes sure as shit didn't add up. He'd have to ask Melissa about it more later. For his own peace of mind.

Maybe he was just a middle-aged, balding guy with a crush on the hot realtor, but Tyler would feel better after he looked into him further.

He walked ahead of the man with a couple of long strides and opened the front door, calling out as he entered. "Hi honey, I'm home!"

Melissa came strutting into the foyer, her sky-high heels clicking on the floor. The smirk on her face nearly had him chuckling, but as she came toward him, looking sexy as sin, his groin tightened.

"You made it on time, snookums," she said, pursing those pretty pink lips of hers as she flipped her red hair over one slender shoulder. Her suit jacket had been tossed off to the side somewhere, and all she had on was a sexy little camisole with that snug skirt. Her full breasts bounced as she walked, the slender straps of her top looking like they would barely hold up, and he resisted the urge to groan in appreciation. "What's the occasion?" she asked.

He chuffed out a laugh. "Anything for you, beautiful. A man would be a fool to keep you waiting."

"And yet you did exactly that yesterday. Hmmm."

The photographer came hurrying in behind him, and Tyler bristled. "I apologize, Ms. Ford. He hurried ahead of me. I would've insisted that I come inside first."

Melissa waved him off, looking annoyed. "It's fine. Tyler is a friend of a friend. Practically like a pesky brother or something."

Tyler moved closer to her, his eyes heating. "A brother?" he asked in a low voice. His gaze raked over her, taking in once more the camisole stretching across her full breasts, the slim skirt she had on, and those mile-long legs, clad in stilettos. "I'm having some very unbrotherly thoughts right now."

She laughed, the rich, throaty sound sending heat

surging through him. "Didn't you read my text earlier?" she asked sweetly. "I'm not sleeping with you." She smiled as she looked up at him, holding his gaze just a beat too long, and then she moved around him, purposefully brushing against him as she walked toward the photographer, who was still waiting in the foyer.

Tyler turned to watch her cross the room, enjoying the way her snug skirt hugged her ass.

Holy hell.

Was there a part of this woman that wasn't as hot as hell?

"All set?" she asked the photographer brightly. "I thought you'd already headed out. I'll just copy the photos to my computer and upload them right now since you're still here. The listing is going live tonight. Unless Tyler here decides to make an offer of course."

"I got everything you asked for," the photographer said, beginning to look slightly flustered as she got closer. He patted his camera nervously.

"Wonderful. Can I pop the thumb drive into my laptop now? It shouldn't take long to copy over the images."

"Well, I should go through all the photos first," he stammered. "Some might need editing and—"

"Nonsense," she declared. "I work with you because you're the best. I've got houses to show Tyler this afternoon and a full schedule. I need to get this uploaded now while I have a place to sit and work."

"Let me just, ah, check on a few things," he said, finally regaining his composure. "I need to make a backup of my photos first—I'm sure you understand."

"Fine," she said, beginning to look annoyed. "I'll be over here reviewing the listings with Tyler."

Tyler raised his eyebrows as she walked back toward him, and she flipped her red hair over her shoulder, rolling her eyes. Tyler was behind her in an instant, pulling out the barstool to help her get seated. She smelled of some exotic floral scent, and his groin tightened. His hands lingered a moment too long on her hips as he helped her climb up, and his gaze briefly shot to her cleavage.

Holy hell.

She settled in, crossing her legs in those stilettos. Her snug skirt pulled across her creamy thighs, and he resisted the urge to groan. To push into her space, spreading her legs wide as he edged between them. As the skirt had nowhere to go but up, revealing whatever sexy little panties she had on.

Jesus Christ.

Looking at houses all afternoon with her was akin to torture. How was a guy supposed to look but not touch when she was the sexiest thing he'd ever seen? When she kept shooting him flirty glances, knowing exactly what she was doing.

She was a tease, and he loved every damn second of it.

He grabbed his own barstool, casting a fleeting glance over to the photographer. The sooner that guy was out of here, the better. Not that anything was going to happen with Melissa, but he'd didn't need a third wheel hanging around. "I think someone has the hots for the gorgeous realtor," he said in a low voice.

"I know you do, sweetie. I'll do my best to ignore it and keep things professional between us."

He chuffed out a laugh, running a hand through

his cropped hair. "Jesus. Let's just get to it then."

She innocently adjusted her camisole, her lips quirking in a smile as his gaze fell on her gorgeous breasts. "I'm not going to fuck you," she said.

"Such a mouth on you, beautiful. Let's get to it, as in show me the homes you want to drag me off to this afternoon."

Melissa shot him a pointed look. "Drag you off? Let's not forget that I'm the one doing you a favor by showing you these listings. It's more like you taking me off on your little adventure."

"Hell, I like the sound of that. I'll take you anywhere you want to go, beautiful."

"Hawaii, perhaps?" she commented, not missing a beat as she pulled up the specs on some properties. "I refuse to set foot in Bora Bora, as I'm sure you understand."

"Your ex was an asshole," Tyler said quietly. "Not that I plan on getting married anytime soon, but if I proposed? I sure as shit wouldn't leave a woman standing at the altar."

"Technically, he didn't. He told me ahead of time."

"Same damn thing," Tyler said. "You were planning a wedding and a life together. Hell, my parents have been married for thirty years. I take things like that seriously. Proposing to a woman and then calling it off? That's a dick move."

"You don't need to tell me twice," she said. "But I thought you were all about sleeping with lots of different women?"

He lifted a shoulder in an easy shrug. "Nothing wrong with that if the woman knows it's just for one night. It's not like I'm asking them to go steady," he said, the corner of his mouth quirking up.

"How romantic," she said sarcastically.

"I've gotten no complaints."

"Here are the photos, Ms. Ford," the photographer said, interrupting them, as he walked over. His face was flushed, with beads of perspiration along his forehead, and Tyler narrowed his gaze.

"Are you feeling all right?"

"Great," he said. "Just trying to wrap everything up before I head out. I know Ms. Ford is busy."

"Wonderful, thanks," Melissa said, taking the thumb drive from him and inserting it into her laptop. She quickly copied over the photos without looking through them. "You're a lifesaver for getting everything done this morning." She pulled out the drive and handed it back to him.

"My pleasure," he said, dabbing his forehead with a tissue. "If you need anything else, I'm happy to come back and meet you again. Maybe this evening?"

"These will be perfect, I'm sure," she said, sliding down off the barstool. Tyler lightly gripped her arm to steady her, her smooth skin under his fingertips nearly sending him up in flames. He'd love to have her naked and writhing beneath him, with all her soft skin and delectable curves his to explore. A woman like her was probably a wildcat in bed. Although he was used to being the one in control, he wouldn't mind letting her have some fun.

At least some of the time.

"Let me walk you to the door," she said, her heels clicking on the floor.

Some of the time?

What the hell was he thinking? He'd spend a night or two with a woman and then move on.

A minute later, Melissa was locking the front door

behind the photographer, sashaying across the room. "Goodness. He's getting to be a hassle to work with. Did I tell you he called me three or four times this morning?"

"No, but he did," Tyler said with a smirk as he crossed his arms. Melissa's gaze slid over his muscled biceps, and warmth surged within him. Maybe she acted unaffected, but he'd caught her watching him as well. "He seemed annoyed that you texted me but didn't return his calls."

Melissa closed her laptop and then grabbed her blazer and slid it on, flipping her red hair over it. Something about the combination of her with those flowing red locks and a business suit did it for him. He wanted to bend her over the nearest surface and thrust into her, not stopping until she was screaming in ecstasy.

"I'm not surprised," she said, sliding her laptop into her bag. "I may need to find someone else to work with. Come in, take the required photos, and get out. Not someone so clingy they need lengthy phone chats before our appointments. Anyway, I can work on the photos for this listing later on. Shall we get going?"

"Absolutely."

"Which home were you interested in seeing first?" She continued going over the options of which listing to start with so they weren't driving back and forth all over town, and he pulled open the front door. Tyler watched as she fiddled with the lockbox after locking up, and then she was taking her car keys from her purse.

"I can drive," he said, taking her arm to help her walk down the front steps.

"Such a gentleman," she teased.

"I'm having very ungentlemanly thoughts," he quipped. "Do you always wear stilettos to show homes, or is that just for my benefit?"

"Well aren't you arrogant. What makes you think I dress for a man?'

He chuckled, clicking the remote to unlock his SUV. "I don't think you dress for a man. I think you dress that way because you enjoy the attention."

"There's nothing wrong with looking good," she said, climbing up into his SUV. Unable to resist, he grabbed the seatbelt and leaned over to buckle it for her, inhaling that sexy floral scent she had on. Letting his hands linger just a beat too long at her waist.

"You'll get no complaints from me," he said, chuckling at the shocked look on her face. Then he reluctantly pulled back, shutting the passenger side door.

Chapter 7

"Want to grab something to eat?" Tyler asked several hours later as they got back into his SUV. He pulled the driver side door shut and started the engine.

"Are you asking me out?" she teased.

"Wouldn't dream of it. I'm just starving." He grinned, his green eyes gleaming in the sunlight. He slid on his aviators and shifted the vehicle into gear, pulling out onto the street. It had been interesting looking at homes today with him. Melissa had expected him to be teasing her all afternoon like he had yesterday, but he seemed genuinely interested.

Funny that a guy like him wanted a huge place to himself. Most of the guys stationed at Quantico just rented like he had been. Even families were known to rent because they'd be here for a year or two and then on to the next assignment.

He didn't seem old enough to want to settle down. Then again, Amy's boyfriend Jason had talked of buying a place, too. He was a little older than them though and was already divorced with a kid.

"Fine," she said. "Let's grab lunch. We can go over the places we saw and decide if you'd like to put an offer in on any of them. Let's pick up my SUV first and then meet at a restaurant."

"Sure thing, beautiful," he said, signaling before he turned onto the main road.

He looked so calm, cool, and collected while driving. Tyler was a man that nothing seemed to faze. If a meteor crashed in front of them, he'd probably just swerve around it, then continue on his way. Although she appreciated someone calm and steady since she was usually racing around in a million different directions, a man like him would never be right for her.

Ever.

She'd done the deployments with her ex, waiting while he was off saving the world.

Giving up on their future.

Melissa studied Tyler as she glanced over—strong profile, aviators concealing his eyes, broad shoulders and bulging biceps. Blond hair cropped short in the standard military fashion. His lips quirked as he glanced over and she didn't look away. "See something you like?" he asked.

"Hmmm," she said, noncommittally.

He chuckled. "No smart comeback?"

"I was actually thinking about the homes we saw. Did any in particular interest you? I can pull more specs this evening, and we can visit a few this week or next weekend. Of, if you want to put in an offer, we can do that as well."

"I thought you wanted to discuss it over lunch."

"Just planning ahead."

Tyler pulled into the driveway of the first home they'd looked at, right beside her SUV. She felt a brief pang in her heart as she glanced at the house—like some sort of strange déjà vu, which was bizarre. Tyler had never driven her anywhere before.

They'd never parked their vehicles next to each other in the driveway.

Maybe it just felt like when she and her ex had been together. They'd pull into one of their places, their cars beside one another, ready to head in and have dinner or snuggle up beside one another for the night.

He'd taken all that from her—their life, their future.

She was supposed to be married and living with him. Happily ever after and all that. Now she wasn't even sure if she believed in that anymore. Maybe her best friends were happy with their guys, but as for her?

Maybe it just wasn't in the cards.

"Hey, did you ever hear from your sister?" Tyler asked, shutting off the engine. He glanced over at her, and she couldn't see his eyes behind his aviators.

"No, but I'm waiting for her to call me. I'm guessing she didn't sleep well last night, so if she crashed, I don't want to wake her up. Especially with the time difference."

"Makes sense," he said. "I'll help you out."

"There's no need," she said, unbuckling her seat belt and opening the passenger door. She slid out, feeling Tyler's gaze on her bare legs. Unwilling to let him know he affected her, she reached in and grabbed her bag without glancing at him. Standing up in her sky-high stilettos, she shut the door.

It was funny seeing his black SUV next to her pristine white one. Yin and yang. Tyler seemed to let nothing affect him, while she was always in a hurry. But she had a huge workload and too much on her plate to live a laidback life like him.

Digging her keys from her bag, she clicked the key fob, opening her own door.

Tyler unrolled the window, and she looked over at him. "Follow me," she said, not giving him the chance to say a thing. "I know a great spot for us to eat."

He nodded, watching as she climbed into her own vehicle. "Sure thing, gorgeous."

She felt heat rising within her, and she calmly shut her door. Weird how suddenly she felt so damn sad. It had been fun looking at homes with Tyler, surprisingly. He'd kept her laughing all afternoon, and if she was honest, it didn't exactly hurt to look at him.

The man was gorgeous.

Muscles upon muscles, chiseled good looks, and a cocky personality that didn't take things too seriously.

Taking a chance on him would be playing with fire though. Maybe he'd hinted that he wanted to sleep with her, but that didn't mean a guy like him wanted a relationship. And she sure wasn't about to get burned again.

***

An hour later, they were tucked into a booth, digging into their food at a trendy restaurant in town. Melissa took a sip of her Bloody Mary before digging into her Eggs Benedict.

"Brunch all day Sunday—I like it," Tyler said.

"More establishments should get on board with this type of thing."

"You don't work Sunday mornings, so what's the need for that?"

"Didn't say I busy working," he said with a low chuckle.

She nearly choked on her food. Of course he meant he was still in bed. Mostly likely with the flavor of the week. He'd probably spend all morning with a woman and then drag her off to eat late in the day.

Goodness.

She was up and meeting with clients, holding open houses, and getting things done. She did have the luxury of sleeping in during the week, but wow.

It was like he loved trying to egg her on and surprise her.

"Hell, I wasn't with anyone this morning, beautiful. Don't look so shocked."

"I still can't believe you can eat all that and stay in shape," she said, gesturing toward his full plate. A huge omelet, stack of pancakes, bacon, and toast nearly spilled over.

He chuffed out a laugh, taking a large bite of his omelet. "I went for a long run this morning. I'm famished. And protein is good for you. I work hard to stay in shape, yes, but I need fuel for that kind of workout."

"Fuel," she said, shaking her head.

"Calories. Energy. Food. I've eaten damn MREs on deployment—it doesn't have to taste good, but your body needs energy."

"Don't you guys train on base a lot? Why were you out running on a Sunday morning?"

"Yep, we do. Doesn't mean I don't work out on

the weekends though. Lifting, running. I did around ten miles earlier before I met you to house hunt. I probably would've hit the gym if we weren't looking at homes."

"That's sounds awful," she said, wrinkling her nose.

"I'm a Marine. You should be used to that with your ex. We train hard."

"Ugh, don't mention him. Running into him last night was bad enough."

"Done," he said with a chuckle.

She raised her eyebrows.

"I've got no interest in talking about your ex with you. What's done is done. His loss." He shrugged, taking another bite of his food.

Melissa watched him for a beat, trying to clear her head. Despite his flirting, he was rather no-nonsense when it came right down to it. With a guy like him, you always knew what he was thinking. Where he stood.

For better or worse.

She resisted the urge to laugh. There'd certainly be no "for better or worse" with him. At least she knew Tyler wasn't interested in settling down. In a commitment. He might flirt every chance that he got, but at least a woman knew what she was in for.

"Amy's a preschool teacher and runner," she said. "It's not just Marines who like to work out you know." She took a bite of her Eggs Benedict, savoring the taste. "God, this is divine. I shouldn't have skipped breakfast this morning."

He watched her for a moment, amused. "Who said I like to work out? I gotta stay in shape for the job. That, and it doesn't exactly hurt to attract the ladies."

Melissa rolled her eyes. "Always back to you and your women."

He chuckled. "I'm single. A red-blooded American male. I'm not going to deny that I like being with a beautiful woman."

"How charming."

"And you dress like that for yourself?" he asked with a smirk, his gaze dropping to her cleavage. She felt warmth rising within her. "Are you saying you don't enjoy spending the night with a man?"

"There's nothing wrong with looking good," she said, stiffening. "And whether or not I enjoy being with a man isn't any of your damn business either. That's personal."

"Maybe you've been with the wrong men."

"I'm selective about who I date—so what. There's nothing wrong with that."

"And hell if I don't appreciate a woman who knows what she wants."

Melissa shrugged, meeting his gaze. His green eyes bore into her, almost as if they could see her very soul. Which was absurd. She'd just met this guy. And they were having a business lunch of sorts. Brunch. Lunch. Whatever.

They didn't need to discuss their dating history or anything. This was strictly business.

Her phone buzzed in her bag, and she frowned as she read the text.

"Everything all right?" Tyler asked.

"Just my sister—still no news. I guess I thought they'd have some sort of update by now."

"That sucks," Tyler said. "I hate to say it, but usually if guys are missing like that, it's not good. If they were hunkered down somewhere, the others would know. I mean it is possible to go radio silent, but they'd be working their way back to base if they could. There'd be teams out looking for them. Chances are, if they were all right, there'd be signs of them."

She blew out a sigh. "Yeah, I figured it wasn't a good thing. But we still have to hold onto some hope, you know? I mean, that's all we have right now."

"Touché. Jason wasn't able to find out anything?"

"No. Part of me hoped that Brody's commander was just keeping us in the dark. It sounds like they really don't know anything though." She shrugged, pushing those thoughts aside. "I'll call my sister later to chat. Let's talk about houses—that's why we're here, right?"

"I have to hand it to you—you really did your research. All the houses we saw were fantastic possibilities. And hell, the prices aren't bad down here, either. An old buddy of mine was trying to buy a home up near the Pentagon. Somewhere in Arlington." He let out a low whistle. "If I wanted to buy a house up there, I'd have to go in with a couple of my closest friends."

"The housing market in Northern Virginia and DC is insane. It's certainly much more affordable down here. So, any thoughts? We can keep looking, make an offer…."

"The first one I saw was the best. That's my preference. I suppose we could look some more, but I don't think it'll be any better than that one."

"It was amazing, right?" she said, nodding enthusiastically. "We can get an offer written up if you want to move on it. I'd recommend asking price at least if you're serious. It's possible they'll get other offers once the listing is live. If we put an offer in tonight, they might accept it though. It's somewhat of a unique situation with my being the buying and selling agent."

"Does that happen a lot?"

"No. It's called dual agency. Really, Amy just happened to mention you needed a Realtor right when I was getting ready to list it. The buyers are interested in making the sale as painless as possible. You buying the property isn't contingent on any sales, which is a plus in this market. People want a sure thing. And with your financials? It'll be a clean contract."

Tyler nodded. "Hell, who would've have thought it? Me, a home owner."

"Everybody has to grow up someday," she joked.

Tyler crossed his arms as he leaned back, looking amused. "I assure you I'm quite grown up, gorgeous. I could show you sometime if you're interested."

"Let's keep things professional," she chided.

"If you insist." He smirked, letting his gaze roam over her. Doing funny things to her insides.

"You won't be sorry," she said, trying to stay on focus. "That house was amazing. And I won't need to list it if they're willing to accept the offer ahead of time."

"Fantastic. So what do we need to do?"

"We'll head into my office," she said. "Write up the papers, and I'll get them to the sellers. If all goes well, they can accept the offer tonight. If not, you can counteroffer and we'll see what they say."

"I got it," Tyler said easily as the waitress brought over their check.

"But you're my client," Melissa protested, reaching

out to grab the billfold from him.

Tyler whisked it out of her reach, chuckling. "I'm not letting a woman buy me brunch. No way."

She playfully swatted his hand, feeling the veins that stood out on his skin. He was solid. Warm. Real. And definitely not someone she should be attracted to. Not at all. "Well aren't you sexist," she countered.

"A simple thank you will suffice."

She rolled her eyes as he pulled out some money and folded it into the billfold.

Chapter 8

Tyler sauntered into the sports bar in town later that evening, taking in the packed tables and bar. A loud roar sounded inside as the crowd cheered at the football game on TV, and there were lots of whoops and hollers.

Braden looked up from his barstool, smirking as Tyler approached. He took a pull from his long neck. "Late for a Sunday night game, bro? What the fuck?"

Tyler glanced up at one of the massive screens, noting the score. He looked back at his buddy. "I looked at houses all afternoon, dude. You know I need a new place to live. I put in an offer on one."

Braden guffawed, elbowing Liam. "Did you hear that?"

"Missed it," Liam said, glancing away from the TV screen. "What's up?"

"I put in an offer on a house," Tyler said, grabbing a barstool. He gestured to the bartender for a beer and grabbed one of the hot wings his buddies had ordered. "I need to move out of my apartment, stat, so I'm looking to buy."

Liam let out a low whistle. "Hell. You need a place so you're buying one? What's next? A wife and couple of kids?"

Tyler chuckled. "Maybe I'm just tired of moving around and having a damn landlord all the time. I had base housing back in Colorado, but I was renting then, too. I'm ready for something different."

"You don't think you'll re-up when it's time?"

"Negative. I've done my duty to Uncle Sam. I can do without the frequent deployments and military chain of command. The moving around."

Braden nodded. "I hear ya. It gets damn old after a while. But what the hell would you do after the Marines?"

Tyler shrugged, taking a pull of the beer the bartender set down in front of him. "Maybe contracting for the Defense Department. Personal training if I'm totally done with the government. I could commute up to the Pentagon, but who the hell knows. I've gone up there for meetings and traffic is hell."

Braden grinned at a group of women hovering near them. "Would you ladies like to join us?"

"Sure thing," one of them said with a smile. "I'm Courtney."

"Well come on over, sweetheart," Braden said, wrapping his arm around her shoulders as she willingly snuggled up next to him. "You want my barstool?"

"Buy me a drink?" she asked, smiling at him.

Liam and Tyler made room for the other women as Braden gestured to the bartender, Tyler's mind drifting toward Melissa. Usually he'd be all over flirting with a pretty woman for an hour or so. Seeing how long it took to convince her to go home with him.

But now?

His head just wasn't in the game.

"Are you stationed at Quantico?" one of the women asked him, reaching out and brushing her fingers over his bicep.

He smirked, appraising her. "Yes, ma'am."

"Oh, don't call me ma'am," she said. "That makes me feel old."

He chuckled, glancing down at his phone. He was hoping to hear back from Melissa about the offer they'd put in. She thought they might have news later tonight.

"Are you ignoring me?" the woman teased.

"Just waiting to hear back from someone," he said in a low voice.

He was waiting to hear about the house, sure. But these women also had him imagining Melissa's flowing red hair and killer curves.

"Well I'm someone," she said suggestively. "We could go somewhere quieter if you prefer. Maybe back to my place?"

Tyler's chest tightened. Hell. The last thing he wanted to do was leave with this woman. Funny, because usually he'd be chasing after a woman like that. Interested in a quick and easy lay.

But now?

Not a fucking chance.

Braden climbed off of his barstool, pulling the woman near him even closer. "We're heading out."

Tyler raised his eyebrows.

"We're going to her place. Sorry to miss the rest of the game, but you understand."

The woman giggled like he'd said the funniest thing in the world, and then she said goodbye to her friends. Tyler watched them walk out, eventually letting his gaze fall back on the TV.

"So that's it? You don't want to sleep with me?"

"Not tonight, sweetheart," Tyler said. "I am waiting to hear back from someone. And I'm here to watch the game."

She pouted, linking arms with her friend who was standing near Liam. "Let's go find another group of guys."

Liam shot him a look as they walked away. "What the hell, man? Just because you weren't interested didn't mean you needed to scare them off."

Tyler shrugged. "So chase after them. Where's everyone else anyway?"

Liam looked over at him, before he was drawn back to the game. "Jason's with Amy tonight—no surprise," he said, taking a swig of his beer as he watched the other team score a touchdown. "And while you were off house hunting with the hot realtor, Grayson met a woman at the gym. I think they drove out to the lake in his truck."

"It's freezing out," Tyler said with a chuckle. "Why the hell would they go out there tonight?"

"I don't think they're planning to leave his truck," Liam said, smirking. "They wanted to have a little privacy."

"And what do you mean I was spending time with the 'hot realtor.' How the hell do you know what Melissa looks like anyway?" Tyler asked.

Liam chuffed out a laugh. "I've seen her around

with Amy before—amazing curves, pouty lips, that long red hair. She was pretty put off on Marines when I met her though. I think she'd just broken up with her ex or something."

"She's off limits," Tyler said gruffly.

"Didn't say I was interested, did I?" Liam said. "I've got a thing for blondes. You seem awfully protective of a woman you're supposedly just working with."

"Didn't say I wasn't interested, did I?" Tyler quipped.

Liam shook his head, laughing. "You're playing with fire. She's not interested in anyone right now, from what I gather. And if you're serious about buying a place, do yourself a favor and don't fuck the realtor."

Tyler clenched his jaw. "What I do and with who is none of your damn business."

Liam shrugged. "I'm just saying don't screw it up."

Tyler's phone buzzed on the bar, and he grabbed it, glancing down at the screen.

They want to think over your offer tonight.
We'll know more tomorrow.

Tyler grumbled to himself, thumbing a response.

This is more stressful than deploying.

He laughed at her text.

Welcome to my world.
I'll have to list the property tonight as planned.

Tyler swiped the screen, calling her. "You still have to list it?" he asked in disbelief.

"And hello to you, too. I'm acting as the buying and selling agent. If they want to move forward and potentially get other offers, I have to honor their wishes. That's not saying you can't put in a counteroffer though. Or wait to see if they decide to accept your initial one."

"Shit," he muttered. "I wasn't expecting buying a place to be do damn stressful."

"Some people put in multiple offers before theirs gets accepted. That's the nature of buying a home. Unless you're willing to pay significantly over asking price, we'll have to wait and see what they say."

"Then we wait," he said, turning his empty beer bottle around in his hand.

"Where are you?" she asked. "It sounds really loud."

"Sports bar. I met some of my buddies from base to watch the game. One of them already ditched us for a woman he met."

Melissa laughed. "Goodness. He moves fast just like you."

"I'm not with a woman now, am I?" Tyler muttered.

"How should I know?"

"That's a negative, beautiful."

She laughed, the sound doing funny things to his libido. "But you were late yesterday morning because you were. You expect me to think you've changed in a day? Not a chance." He could practically hear the smile in her voice, and Tyler's chest tightened. Who the hell was he kidding? She was spot on about him.

"I'll call you tomorrow, Romeo," she teased. "Don't get into too much trouble."

She disconnected the call, and Tyler was left gazing at the phone in his hands.

"Bad news?" Liam asked, raising his eyebrows.

Tyler cleared his throat. "Still no word on the house. They should let me know tomorrow."

"Well drink up, then. No sense in worrying about it now. Bartender!" he called out, gesturing for another round. Tyler's gaze fell on the other side of the bar, where the women from earlier had found a new set of guys to flirt with. He should go over there. Take one of them home for the night. Lose himself in a beautiful woman for a few hours.

Funny how he didn't feel like doing any of that though.

Chapter 9

Melissa flipped her hair over her shoulder, crossing her legs at the table she was seated at in the coffee shop a few days later. She took a sip of her steaming hot latte, savoring the taste and the accompanying jolt of espresso. Tyler had texted her at six in the morning, no doubt on his way into base, but she could've done without the early morning wake up call.

Not that he'd seen a problem with it.

This was her third cup of coffee already, and she'd probably need more to get through her jam-packed day.

She adjusted her trendy off-the-shoulder sweater, smiling as a man glanced her way as he headed out the door. Wearing her pale pink sweater paired with her snug dark-wash jeans and knee-high boots, she felt sexy and sophisticated.

Not to mention more comfortable than prancing around in those power suits and sky-high heels.

Still, she had an image to maintain. She liked to

look her best showing homes. If wearing business suits with stilettos made her feel powerful and put together—not to mention sexy and in control—then so be it.

Tyler certainly hadn't complained.

Her phone buzzed on the table, and her eyes widened as she saw that it was the sellers of the home Tyler had put an offer in on. "Hello?" she said, lifting her cell to her ear.

"Hi Melissa. We've decided to go ahead and accept Tyler's offer. What's the next step we need to take to move forward?"

Melissa grinned. "Fantastic," she said. "I can meet you in the office to sign the papers. Tyler's on base, but I'll try to get a hold of him and see if he can meet me, too. Once both parties have signed and are in agreement, we'll set up a settlement date."

"Wonderful. At first we had wanted to see what other offers came in after listing the home, but after some consideration, we decided to go ahead with his offer."

"I understand," Melissa said smoothly. "Once the papers are signed today, I'll take the listing down. We can take the lockbox off the door, too."

"I'm so sorry," the woman gushed. "I know you worked hard to get it photographed and listed over the weekend. We just didn't know what we wanted to do."

"It's no problem. That's my job," Melissa assured her. "Goodness, I've listed some houses only to have the seller change their mind and take it off the market."

"That's horrible!"

"Nature of the job," Melissa said, taking another

sip of her latte. "Some have second thoughts about selling, some decide to rent. Sometimes a job offer or something falls through and they end up not moving."

"Goodness, I can't imagine. We'll sign the offer papers and get them to you right away. Can I leave them at the office if you're not there?"

"Of course. I'll get in touch with Tyler, and then we'll be all set."

"Fantastic. Talk to you soon."

The women said their goodbyes, and Melissa flipped her laptop shut. So much for getting a lot of work done here. She grabbed her suede jacket, slipping it on over her pale pink sweater. Packing up her things, she grabbed her latte and headed for the door.

***

Melissa looked up as Tyler sauntered into her office a couple of hours later, trying not to stare. He had on a tee shirt that showed off his muscular arms and khaki cargo pants, his green eyes gleaming in amusement as he watched her.

"What's so funny?" she asked with a frown.

"You. Ogling me."

"I wasn't ogling you," she protested, a feeling of warmth surging through her.

He smirked, coming to a stop at her desk. "I don't mind, beautiful. A gorgeous woman like you, looking at me like that? It's not exactly a hardship." His gaze roamed over her, his lips quirking. "I was trying to figure out what looks different about you today, and I just got it—no suit or stilettos."

"I hadn't planned on any meetings today," she said smoothly. "I was working remotely from the coffee shop in town."

His eyes landed on her bare shoulder. "I like this look," he said in a low voice. "It's—softer on you."

"I'm not soft," she scoffed.

He chuckled. "I beg to differ. But I don't want to get in too much trouble," he added with a wink. "This is an office, not a date."

Melissa rolled her eyes, standing up from her desk. She was even shorter without her stilettos on, barely coming up to Tyler's shoulder as she rounded the desk. She forced herself to look up and meet his gaze. "I didn't realize you dated."

"Date. Flirt. Call it what you want. My thoughts still aren't appropriate for this venue."

"Not surprising," she said dryly as he chuckled. "Here are the papers. Just sign where I've marked, and I'll take the listing down from the database. We'll get an appraisal and settlement date and be all set."

"Sounds great," he said, grabbing a pen from her desk and bending over to sign the documents. He scrawled his signature at the bottom and then stood up, gazing down at her. "So that's it? Seems a little anticlimactic."

She laughed despite herself. "Should we have balloons and a parade after your settlement? Maybe try to get it made into a national holiday or something?"

"Hell yeah. I worked damn hard to buy a place of my own. After moving around all the time? Spending years going wherever the military says? It feels good to say that I'll finally have my own home. I'm not much into decorating and that girly shit, but I'll set up a monster grill out back, have my buddies over—be all set."

"I can understand wanting somewhere to call your own. Especially after moving around and deploying a lot. You don't think you'll get sent somewhere after this assignment though?"

"Negative. I'm not planning to re-up."

"Oh," she said, surprised. That changed things in a way. She'd assumed he'd eventually want to rent or sell when he moved on. But to find out he was really planning to stay?

Wow.

"I assume you own your own place?" he asked.

"You assume correctly. It's somewhat rare to find a realtor not interested in real estate. Many own multiple properties—rentals and what not."

"You could start your own show like that couple on TV—flip houses or something."

"And move out to the west coast?" she asked, wrinkling her nose. "No thanks. What's so funny anyway?" She cocked her head to the side as he chuckled, his green eyes sparking with amusement.

"You. It's cute as fuck when you wrinkle your nose like that."

"I'm not soft, and I'm most definitely not cute."

"You're attractive as hell, Melissa," he said with a laugh. "But sometimes? Yeah. Definitely cute as fuck."

"Well, don't let the word get out," she said, crossing the room to make copies of the documents. "Real estate can be a cut-throat business. That's why you always see me in suits when I'm showing homes. I have to keep up a professional demeanor."

"I don't mind this look," he said, his eyes heating

as she crossed the room back toward him. "So what are you doing this afternoon anyway?"

"What do you mean, what am I doing? I'm working. Same as most people, I suppose."

"No way. Not any more you're not. We're going out to celebrate."

"Celebrate? We haven't settled yet."

"They accepted my offer. That's damn good news to me. And hell, I've been on base since six-thirty this morning."

"Don't I know it," she muttered, rounding her desk to file the papers.

"What? You didn't appreciate my early morning text? I just wanted an update before heading in."

"I think maybe you just enjoy torturing me."

"That too," he agreed, not missing a beat. "But I'm not going back to the office on a beautiful day like this. No way. It may be winter, but the sun's out. Come on. Lock up or whatever you need to do. Shut down your laptop. We're heading out."

"We?"

"Yeah, we. I don't bite. Not unless you want me to that is," he added with a grin.

"You're impossible. And where would we be going exactly?" she asked.

"It's a surprise."

"And I'm supposed to trust you?"

Those green eyes nailed her with another heated haze, and her heart unexpectedly fluttered. He took a step toward her, knowing he had her. Knowing she'd do whatever he wanted. "Implicitly."

Chapter 10

Tyler glanced over at Melissa as they drove down the road heading out of town, amazed that she'd agreed to go somewhere with him. Not that he thought she didn't trust him. They had mutual friends, for God's sake. But he was sure he'd have to do a hell of a lot more convincing to get her out of the office.

There was light traffic this time of afternoon, and with the sun shining and bright blue sky, it was one of those days that sucked to be in the office.

Which was why he wasn't headed back.

His buddies on base assumed he'd be a while at Melissa's office. And the fact that he was now cruising around with a beautiful woman at his side?

They'd be none the wiser.

She flipped her red hair over her shoulders, some of that exotic floral scent she had on wafting his way, and he resisted the urge to groan.

Driving around with her in an enclosed vehicle was more brutal than basic training—it took everything in his power not to reach over and tug her closer. Haul her into his arms. He'd seen that creamy porcelain skin on her bare shoulders in that sexy little sweater she had on. It didn't exactly seem like it would keep her very warm in the middle of winter, but as far as looking sexy as fuck?

It hit all the marks.

All he'd need to do was push that suede jacket she was wearing aside and he'd be able to run his fingers over her bare skin.

Feel her softness and warmth.

She looked casual yet incredibly sexy today—the woman certainly could wear a pair of jeans. Strutting around in those high-heeled boots of hers, wearing denim that hugged every inch of her curves? That perfectly highlighted her ass?

Melissa all covered up was even sexier than Melissa in those short skirts and stilettos.

And wasn't that saying something.

Although she seemed to be wearing trendy clothes, she didn't seem to realize how damn tempting she was. He was attracted to her without her even trying. A woman like her would look good in everything and nothing at all.

Hell.

He'd love to see her in nothing but lingerie and those stilettos she loved to strut around in.

A woman like her probably wasn't shy about her body. She'd enjoy tempting and teasing him. And wouldn't he fucking love every minute as well.

Still, he had no damn business dragging her away for the afternoon. Taking her down to the lake—a place where he liked to spend some alone time.

What the hell did he expect was going to happen?

They'd hang out for a few hours and life would go on. He'd be back on base tomorrow; she'd be back showing homes, driving around prospective clients. He frowned. The incident from a few weeks ago was niggling at the back of his mind. The BOLO they'd gotten on base. Nothing had been in the news about it since, but that didn't mean it was necessarily safe for her either.

Not until he was caught.

And a single woman couldn't ever be too careful.

"So, you're not going to give me any hints?" she asked, looking around. "Why are we heading out of town anyway?"

"It's a sunny winter day, I've got the afternoon off—I wanted a break. To go somewhere for a change of scenery."

"And that scenery would be…?"

He chuckled. "We're heading to the lake, beautiful. Nothing better than just hanging out by the water. We'll enjoy some peace and quiet and pretend we're not in the middle of the work week. Just relax and enjoy the great outdoors."

"You don't seem like the 'peace and quiet' type."

"I'm full of surprises. You don't seem like the type to run off with a guy you hardly know."

"Touché. But you're not exactly a random stranger or something. I know where you work. I know where you're about to live."

"I know. I just like riling you up, gorgeous. But I want you to know you don't have to worry—you're safe with me."

She glanced over at him, those light green eyes of hers flickering with a hint of vulnerability for a brief moment before her shield was back in place. "I can take care of myself," she said. "I wouldn't have come with you if I didn't feel comfortable."

"I'm sure you can. I'm just letting you know you don't have to worry about me. Speaking of safety—"

"We weren't," she commented dryly, shooting him a look.

He shook his head, glancing back at the road. "Aren't you ever concerned about being alone when showing homes? That photographer of yours was prowling around outside the house. You were working at your laptop and didn't even know he was there."

"Of course I knew he was there. He was photographing the property," she said, blowing out an exasperated sigh. "He gave me the photos, remember? And yes, he's a little annoying. And also completely harmless."

"But you met me, sight unseen, and took me into an empty house."

"That's not my usual practice," she said. "I even explained that when we first met. I was doing Amy and Jason a favor. Usually I meet clients at my office, go over all their papers, get a copy of their driver's license—"

"Have you thought about getting a firearm?" he asked, frowning.

"I have pepper spray. And not that I enjoy talking about my ex, but he did teach me some self-defense moves. You can't date a Marine without that."

"Well that's something," Tyler muttered. Worry churned through his gut, and wasn't that a shock to his system. He took women home all the time. Or met a woman at a bar and went back to her place. He was never concerned about their safety—sure, he wasn't a threat, but he didn't lecture them on their personal safety either. Or tell them not to bring home a man they didn't know.

What was his deal with worrying about Melissa?

"Why are you so concerned anyway?" she asked, echoing his thoughts. "There are lots of realtors around. Women realtors," she clarified. "I mean, you could get kidnapped walking down the street."

Tyler turned to her, raising his eyebrows. "I could get kidnapped."

"Not *you* you. The general you. I doubt anyone would try to grab a Marine off the street. Not anyone with an ounce of sense anyway. But nowhere is completely safe if you're a woman. Someone could grab you in the parking lot, wait in your home. I mean, goodness, Amy jogs those trails in the forest all the time. Jason is with her a lot now, I suppose. But that's not exactly safe either."

"I'm just worried, beautiful."

"Well there's no need to be. Where are we going?" she suddenly shrieked, grabbing his arm as he abruptly pulled off the highway and onto a dirt road. His SUV bounced along, some overgrown bushes brushing against the side of the vehicle until they got into a clearing. Some of the trees around were bare since it was the middle of winter, but the evergreens provided a shot of greenery along the landscape.

With the bright sun overhead and the empty dirt road to the lake ahead of them, he was feeling damn fantastic.

Not to mention that fact that he had a beautiful woman at his side.

"The lake. I told you that."

He slowed as they went over a bump, Melissa

clutching his arm more tightly. "I thought you meant we were taking a paved road. To a big lake or something. Or one of the beach areas by the river. You know, the type of place people usually go to around here?"

Tyler chuckled. "I know what you mean, gorgeous. But this is even better. Trust me."

"How can I trust you when I don't even know where we're going?"

He glanced down at her hand on his arm. Her touch was so soft, he wondered briefly if she felt that soft and smooth all over. If she was still hanging on to him because she liked touching him, too. "Look, beautiful. We're not going camping in the wilderness or something. When you said they'd accepted my offer on the house, I decided to take the afternoon off to celebrate. Hell, my buddies still think I'm at the office with you."

"Fantastic," she said sarcastically, finally releasing him and settling back into her seat. "I do have work to do, you know."

"I didn't see you complaining when we left. And it's not like I dragged you out the door or something. Live a little."

"Is that the new Marine motto? Live a little?"

He chuckled. "Hell, I've been deployed to the Middle East four times. I'm lucky as hell to have made it back. Speaking of which, what ever happened with your sister's boyfriend?"

"Fiancé," Melissa said, stiffening. "And he's still missing. It's only been a few days, but I have a bad feeling. I wanted to fly out there to be with Becky, but she's just starting a new semester. She told me not to come yet." Melissa shrugged. "It sucks, but what am I supposed to do? She's a big girl. She's just waiting to hear more and holding onto hope."

"You're doing what you can," he assured her.

They finally reached a small group of trees, and Tyler pulled through them, coming to a stop at a secluded lake. The sun glistened on the water, and he let out an appreciative whistle. "What did I tell you? Gorgeous on a day like today."

"How did you find this place? Is it on someone's property?"

"Technically yes, but it's owned by the relatives of a buddy of mine. They said I could come here anytime I wanted."

"Wow." She looked around, relaxing slightly in her seat. "It looks…nice."

He chuckled. "Why do you sound surprised?"

"It just feels like we're in a different place. I mean, it's right outside of town, but it's secluded and out of the way. Kind of like a secret little hideaway."

He shut off the engine, opening the driver's side door. "I hear ya. Kind of like getting away without getting away. I come down here as often as I can when I just need some time to myself."

Tyler shut his door, frowning as Melissa climbed out of the passenger side herself. Not that he went around wining and dining women, but he had basic manners. There was nothing wrong with helping a woman in and out of his SUV. Holding the door.

Feeling her soft curves against him.

She didn't seem interested in his help though, and in a couple of long strides, he was catching up to where she stood, looking out at the lake. She shivered slightly, and he wished he'd thought ahead to bring something warm.

Or that he was the type of man that carried around a blanket in his trunk.

Not that he'd exactly planned this little outing. It wasn't like he'd woken up expecting to sign papers in her office. Or to bring her along with him on this little adventure.

Melissa glanced around nervously, her gaze scanning the ground. "I hope there's no snakes around here."

"Snakes? I haven't seen any before. Besides, they probably hibernate or something during the winter."

"Or something," she muttered, shivering again. "That's real comforting."

"Hell," he said. "Come here." Not giving her a chance to protest, he pulled her into his arms, so that she was leaning back against his chest. Her smaller frame up against his body was pure heaven. Her head rested perfectly beneath his chin, her backside against his groin, and he resisted the urge to groan.

To do something that would scare her away.

Because right now?

There was something damn right about holding her here. And he was aroused as hell holding her in his arms.

"Do you take all the girls down here?" she teased, nestling against him.

He tightened his grip ever-so-slightly. "Not a single one," he said in a low voice. "I've never brought a woman here before."

She stiffened slightly against him, and he ducked lower, his lips against her red hair. "Relax, beautiful," he said, inhaling her exotic floral scent. Feeling her tremble slightly against him. "I already said I'd never hurt you."

Chapter 11

Melissa's heart pounded in her chest as Tyler nuzzled against her. As his arms tightened slightly around her. His body behind hers was pure heaven—solid and strong and just right. Warm when she was cold, protective in the way that he held her.

But she wasn't looking to be with a man.

Not now.

Not him.

His clean, masculine scent filled the air, and the warmth from him seeped into her, even through their clothes and coats. Her body heated at his nearness, at the strength and power of him holding her. He was both gentle and powerful at the same time—an interesting dichotomy.

A man like Tyler could break her in half if he wanted—and he could protect her from anyone and everyone if needed.

She didn't need a protector though.

And she certainly didn't need to fall into bed with

another man.

"Did you hear me, beautiful?" he asked in a low voice, the deep sound causing her insides to do a funny little flip. "I said I'd never hurt you. I know you were burned by your ex, but I want you to know you'll be safe with me."

"I'm not looking for any sort of relationship right now," she said softly. "It doesn't matter if I'd be safe or not with you—I'm not looking for that."

"Neither was I. But I also know that you're not the type of woman I could take home for a night and then just forget about. You're not the type of woman I could make love to and then never see again. Not when you're on my mind every damn minute."

"Tyler," she protested, edging away slightly. She shouldn't be attracted to him. Not even a little bit. She was barely over her breakup with her ex and certainly didn't need to go from the arms of one Marine to another.

She absolutely didn't need to jump out of the frying pan and into the fire.

He let her go, and she turned to look up at him, hating even the few inches of distance now between them. She shivered at the loss of his warmth, at the chill in the winter air. His green eyes locked on her, and her gaze briefly ran over his chiseled jaw. Took in the slight blond scruff of his five o'clock shadow. The broadness of his shoulders.

She glanced back up to meet his eyes. Eyes that always seemed to see right through her. How could someone she barely even know seem to penetrate her very soul?

"Tell me I'm just like every other guy you've met," he said, his voice gruff. "That you've felt like this before. The chemistry between us is insane."

"We barely even know one another. We just met the other day. This is crazy!"

"Not crazy. Hell, I've been a lot more intimate with women I've known a lot less."

Pain stabbed in her chest as she took a step backward, and hurt and resentment seeped through her. There he was, throwing that in her face again. Reminding her of all the women he'd slept with. She was just another conquest to be claimed. Not that she was looking to settle down and marry the man. Shoot, she wasn't sure if she ever wanted to get married after the catastrophe of her failed engagement. And she'd certainly had her fair share of boyfriends over the years.

But for Tyler to constantly be mentioning the many, many women he'd been with?

Ugh.

Nothing like making her feel like she was just another warm body for him to have in his bed.

Not that she was planning to sleep with him anyway.

He was her client. She was helping him to buy a house, and they'd barely even started the process. She wasn't going to let him take her home for a night and then just sit across from him at settlement and act like everything was okay. Act like that was something she did all the time.

And she sure the hell wasn't going to do it when he kept throwing his casualness with women in her face. Maybe Tyler was used to random hookups and meaningless sex, but she wasn't built that way.

She wasn't looking to run off to Vegas and tie the knot, but she sure the hell wasn't looking for a string of meaningless sex partners either.

She glared at him, trying to ignore the conflicting feelings churning inside of her. One minute she'd felt safe and secure in his arms, like she could relax and be herself with him. And the next? Like just another potential notch on his belt.

One who didn't mean anything more than every other woman he'd been with.

"I think we should head back," she said stiffly.

"Head back? We just got here."

"And then you so sweetly told me yet again about the random women you've slept with."

He looked baffled. "You're missing the whole point. You're not like the women I've been with in the past. I didn't take you home from the bar the other night, I walked you to your car. Made sure you were safe to drive home. I didn't try to get you into bed this afternoon, I brought you out here, someplace I love."

"Well maybe you should be more careful about what you say. You said you have no interest in talking about my ex? What makes you think I want to hear about yours?"

"You almost married the guy," he said, shaking his head. "It's totally different. My past was just—meaningless. Nothing. It doesn't even compare."

He paced back and forth, looking agitated.

"How lovely."

"There you go, shutting me out again," he said, his mouth pressed in a firm line as he turned to look at her again.

She shivered in her suede jacket, wishing she'd worn something warmer. Wishing she was still back in her office. "Tyler, what exactly did you think was going to happen here? We'd drive out here and—what?"

"I was trying to let you know I understand that you've been burned by a guy before. That I won't hurt you. Do I usually move quickly with a woman I'm interested in? Hell yeah. Do I usually try to take her home right away? Absolutely. I'm trying to do the right thing here with you."

"*With* me? I mean—we're not even together. I'm helping you buy a home. We're working together. We're not dating or a couple. We're not anything!"

"And then when settlement's over? You're going to never talk to me again because I'm one of your former clients? Act like you don't feel the electricity between us every time we get near one another? What if we're out at the bar with Amy and Jason. Would you seriously be okay with watching me take another woman home while you're sitting right there?"

"I just—I don't know!" she said, crossing her arms and glaring at him.

"Why put on a show at all? Just admit what you're feeling. Tell me there's nothing between us—that I'm imagining the whole thing. Because it sure as hell didn't feel that way a few minutes ago."

Melissa sighed, looking away from him. "Let's just forget it. Maybe you're taking the rest of the day off to celebrate, but I really have work to do. I've got an open house this weekend, other properties to get listed. I have a career to think about—a life. Coming here together was a mistake."

"Hell. I'm not trying to peel your clothes off or something—not that I'd mind if you offered. Am I attracted to you? Fuck yes. Do I realize you need to take things slowly? That this might never go anywhere? Also a yes."

A slight breeze blew off the lake, ruffling her hair. Tears smarted her eyes, and she turned away from him, not willing to let him see her cry.

Not willing to shed any tears on yet another man.

She squeezed her eyes tightly shut as hot tears began to roll down her cheeks. As she tried to block out everything else around her. She couldn't even turn around and look at him right now.

Couldn't even go anywhere if she wanted.

She needed to pull herself together and get on with her life. Just like she always had before. Just like she always would.

"Shit," Tyler muttered, taking a step closer. "Don't cry," he said softly, a large hand landing on her shoulder. She trembled as she swiped at her tears, waves of embarrassment washing over her. She was a no-nonsense business woman. Someone who didn't take shit from anyone.

And now she was standing here outside with tears streaming down her cheeks?

Shaking as she tried to keep her emotions inside?

She swiped at her tears again, her fingers cold. Why was she crying anyway? Just because he was trying to be nice to her? Maybe he was going about everything the absolute wrong way, but goodness. He was just trying to get to know her.

To show her in his own bumbled way that he cared.

"Just forget it," she whispered.

Before another beat passed, Tyler was pulling her close. Wrapping those muscular arms around her. Holding her against his solid chest.

Her tears wet his jacket, and she gasped, trembling

as emotions seemed to just flood from her. Every emotion she'd been feeling for the past few months seemed to just pour out of her finally—her anger at her ex. Her fear of a new relationship. The way Tyler seemed to see right through the façade she built up and into her very soul.

She barely even knew the man, and he could see that she was frightened.

That she kept a level head in her career, perhaps, but her personal life felt like it was falling apart. His arms were the only thing holding her together right now.

His embrace the only thing keeping her from falling further apart.

"Shhh, baby," he said, his voice deep, a large hand running through her hair. "Shhh. Don't cry."

She shuddered against him, and he held her tightly. Protecting her from the world. Saving her from herself.

It was almost like Tyler could somehow could see right through her and tear down the walls she'd built up around her heart. She swore she'd never be with another military man after Michael had walked out on her.

But now?

Somehow, despite everything, she just wanted to nestle even closer to Tyler. To let him shield her from the rest of the world for a while, safe in his arms.

Which was absolutely insane.

As her tears slowed, she blinked up at him, Tyler's fingertips brushing away the wetness on her cheeks. Before she could question anything or insist again that they leave, he was ducking down, showing her how much he wanted her.

She gasped as his full lips met hers, and then she was clinging to him, desperate. Kissing him like they were always meant to be together.

"You're cold," he said in a low voice, pulling back as she shivered again. "Let's go back to the car."

She nodded, letting him take her hand as they made their way back to the SUV. His calloused fingers felt rough against hers, and she was reminded at how different their lives and careers were. He was a man who'd been sent off to war. Who'd seen things she could never imagine.

Yet at this very moment?

She had a feeling she'd let him lead her anywhere.

Tyler helped her into his SUV, saying he'd turn on the heat, and then he was rounding the front of the vehicle. Climbing inside and turning on the engine.

The heat blasted from the vents as she trembled in the front seat, both from cold and emotion. "Come here," he said, pinning her with his green gaze as he held out a hand.

She turned to face him, hesitating for only a moment, and then he was pushing his seat back and lifting her into his arms. She gasped as she straddled him, his erection digging into her core. Even through their layers of clothes she could feel how much he wanted her.

How hot and hard he was.

His muscular hands wrapped around her hips, holding her to him, and she whimpered as he pulled her closer still. Her hands landed on his broad shoulders, and then he was kissing her. Nipping and tasting and devouring her.

His mouth moved over hers like she was his to claim—like she'd never been truly kissed by a man before.

He didn't hesitantly see what she liked—he consumed her.

The scruff of his whiskers brushed against her tender skin, and then he nipped at her jaw line, forcing her to tilt her head back as she gasped.

Liquid heat pooled within her, and she moaned as she lightly bucked against him. Tyler growled in approval, and then he was gently bucking beneath her, sending desire shooting straight to her clit with every movement.

One hand gripped her waist as the other ran through her hair, holding her to him. His mouth met hers again, commanding and insistent. Demanding she give him more. She parted her lips to his tongue, and then he was tasting her.

Sliding his tongue against hers in a way that let her know exactly what he wanted. That showed her precisely how he'd make love to her, if given the chance.

Melissa shrugged out of her suede jacket, Tyler helping her toss it to the side, and then he was pulling her pale pink sweater up, revealing her to his gaze.

His green eyes heated as he looked at her. As his gaze roamed over her body. "Hell, Melissa, you're gorgeous. Beautiful and feminine and—amazing. So fucking soft and sweet."

Her breasts jutted out in her lacy lavender bra, and he let his hands rest on her ribcage, his thumbs trailing over the top of her bra, caressing her breasts. His calloused thumbs on her bare flesh sent a shiver racing down her spine.

Watching his muscular hands touching her lace-clad breasts was arousing as hell. She wanted those hands everywhere. Running over every inch of her skin.

Sending her entire body up in flames.

"Are you cold?" he asked huskily.

"No," she said, biting her lip as she shook her head. He cupped her breasts, seemingly in awe himself as he looked down at her. She needed his touch everywhere. Running over all the curves of her body. Spreading her legs apart. Parting her lower lips. Touching her swollen folds as he teased and pleasured her.

Tyler brushed her hair back off her shoulder and ducked down, his teeth grazing her neck as she arched against him. "You, speechless?" he asked huskily. "I never thought I'd see the day."

One large hand palmed her breast through her lacy bra, and he kneaded and caressed her, causing her to whimper against him.

"I could never get enough of you," he muttered, kissing and sucking at the flesh on her neck. "Never. You smell like flowers and rain. And you have the body of a goddess."

She whimpered as he nipped at her neck again, his whiskers scratching at her skin. Tyler smelled faintly of aftershave and something else purely male. She felt wanton and reckless sitting astride him in his SUV, wearing her bra, jeans, and heeled boots while he was still fully dressed. There was something masculine and arousing about him wearing a black leather jacket, the contrast of it against her lavender lace bra startling.

He was a powerful man—a Marine.

And she was helpless to his touch.

He tugged the cups of her bra down, growling in approval as her breasts were pushed upward, perfectly on display for him. "You're gorgeous," he murmured. "So soft and pink and perfect." His thumbs trailed back and forth over her nipples, and she gasped, arching her back and inadvertently thrusting her breasts further toward him.

"Can you come if I play with your nipples?" he asked huskily.

The peaked beneath his touch, and she whimpered in delight. "I don't know, I just, I need—"

He undid the clasp of her bra, tossing it aside with her discarded sweater. With one hand supporting her back, the other at the back of her head, he suddenly leaned her backwards, his face at her breasts. There was barely enough room in his SUV, and she could feel the steering wheel at her back. It was slightly uncomfortable, but being in Tyler's arms like this was pure heaven.

He flicked his tongue over one nipple, causing her to writhe on his lap, before blowing on it gently. The contrast of his hot mouth and the cool air was nearly too much to bear. He laved his tongue over her nipple again, nipping and sucking as she squirmed atop him.

As she cried out in surprise.

"Come for me, gorgeous."

Arousal dampened her folds, and she wished she wasn't wearing jeans today of all days. If she'd had on a skirt, he could've easily tugged it up.

Fingered her swollen folds.

Sent her straight to heaven.

But this?

Sitting atop his hard cock, separated by their clothing, was practically too much.

His wicked mouth moved to her other breast, and

he lightly traced his tongue around her areola. She cried out, and he began to lightly flick his tongue over her taut bud, peaks of pure pleasure beginning to burst forth within her. He lightly bit down, causing her to gasp in surprise, and then he was tonguing her again.

Faster. Harder.

Every jolt of electricity was shooting straight to her clit, and as she squirmed again in his arms, he bucked up against her. Again. She was helpless to move from atop him, and then she was coming. Crying out his name in surrender, his mouth still hot on her breast.

She lay flushed and sated in his arms, shocked that he could pleasure her without even so much as touching her pussy.

A smug look of satisfaction crossed his face, and he pulled her back upward, his arms locked around her. "I like you topless," he said, a wicked gleam in his green eyes as he gazed from her flushed face to her full breasts.

"Bastard," she scoffed softly.

"You weren't saying that when you were crying out my name a minute ago."

"Are you sure?" she asked, breathless.

He smirked. "You're so fucking perfect for me, beautiful. I want you any and every way imaginable. All day and all night."

"Perfect for you? We're not even together," she protested.

"We're together in my car. I've got you sitting in my lap—on top of my cock. The only thing better would be if I were inside you. If your hot pussy was clamped down around my rock-hard cock."

She gasped in surprise, and he chuckled. "I want to feel your walls clamping down around me, beautiful. I want to be inside you when you cry out my name in surrender." He lightly ran one hand over a bare breast, watching as she trembled at his touch. "I meant what I said, beautiful. I won't hurt you."

He palmed both breasts, kneading and caressing as he ducked down and kissed her. "I like you like this," he said. "Flushed and sated—and at my complete mercy."

He held his forehead to hers for a brief moment, and then she glanced around the secluded lake before once again meeting his heated gaze. "We should get going. What if someone sees us here? I'm sitting on your lap topless."

"No one's around, beautiful. And I fucking love you topless. But we can go. I want you all to myself." He ducked lower, his lips brushing against her ear. "And I sure as hell don't want anyone seeing what's mine."

"Who says I'm yours?" she taunted.

"You're half naked on my lap, beautiful," he murmured, his breath hot against her. "If I had my way, you'd be completely naked, writhing beneath me."

She squirmed atop him, and he chuckled. "Now you get the picture," he said, his voice gruff. He reached over and grabbed her sweater. "Leave the bra off. I want to see your gorgeous breasts when we're driving back."

She lightly smacked his chest. "Then why wear anything at all?" she said, pulling her sweater down over her head. "I could just forget clothes all together."

He ducked down and kissed her bare shoulder, his fingers trailing over her skin. "Because you're mine, beautiful. I already told you that. And this skimpy sweater is sexy as fuck. I can see your nipples through the material."

"Tyler...."

He helped her climb off him, and she settled into the passenger seat, stuffing her bra into her bag as he chuckled. "You weren't serious about needing to go back into the office, were you?" he asked, raising his eyebrows. "I can think of about a million things more interesting to do together."

"Dead serious. I've got an open house to prep for."

"Well hell."

She pulled her suede jacket back on as he frowned. "Let's get going snookums," she said sweetly. "I've got work to do."

Chapter 12

"Where the hell did you disappear off to today?" Braden asked as Tyler sank down onto a barstool later that night.

He barely glanced up as a woman in a skimpy top reached over him to grab her drink.

"Didn't Liam tell you? Business," he said, gesturing to the bartender for a beer. He scrubbed a hand across the stubble on his jaw, frowning. After he'd dropped Melissa off at her office, he'd driven around aimlessly for an hour. Which sure as shit wasn't like him.

Since when did he get all broody over a woman?

He didn't know what the hell he'd been thinking taking her out to the lake. She wasn't his girlfriend—she wasn't his anything.

And hauling her into his lap like that? Stripping off her top so he could see her perfect breasts, all full and creamy with those gorgeous pink nipples?

Holy hell.

He'd been harder than a rock with her sitting astride him. And he'd wanted nothing more than her pleasure—nothing more than for her to come apart in his arms. To cry out his name. He hadn't even seen her perfect little pussy yet. Hadn't stripped off her panties and touched her silken folds. Tasted her.

"Yo. Earth to Tyler!" Braden said, chuckling.

Tyler glanced down at the beer the bartender had put in front of him. "Just thinking," he muttered.

"So what business kept you off base all afternoon? The house thing?"

He nodded, taking a swig of the hoppy brew. "Yep. The sellers accepted my offer, so I had to sign some papers at Melissa's office. Get the ball rolling, so to speak. I have to be out of my place in a few weeks, so I was glad to find a house that I liked."

"And that took a few hours?"

"Settlement will. This was just signing the paperwork for the offer I put on the house. I took her down with me to the lake for the afternoon—kind of a bad idea, actually."

"Wait—you took a woman with you to the lake? When's the wedding?" he asked, shaking his head in disbelief.

Tyler rolled his shoulders, letting some of the tension ease off of him. "I just wanted to get away for a little bit. I wasn't planning to take her along, it just—happened. It was a gorgeous afternoon; she's a gorgeous woman…." He trailed off.

"So what? You fucked her?"

"No," Tyler growled, anger rising within him. "I didn't fuck her. Jesus."

Even if he had claimed Melissa, he sure as shit wouldn't be telling his buddies about it. He glared at his friend.

"Whoa," Braden said, holding up his hands. "Easy there. You're the guy who's looking for a new woman every week. Who tells the whole damn world about the women you're with. Why the hell would I think she's any different?"

"She's not," he muttered.

Braden chuckled. "Uh-huh. That's why you're so defensive and not telling me all about how many times and ways you had sex with her."

"I didn't sleep with her."

"Exactly," Braden quipped.

Someone cleared his throat behind them, and Tyler glanced up to see Jason listening in, an amused expression on his face. "It sounds like I got here just in time," he joked.

"Where's your better half?" Tyler quipped.

Jason sank onto a barstool, chuckling. "Out with yours."

Braden guffawed. "I knew something was up. You've got a girl; he's got a girl. Tyler just doesn't want to admit it yet."

Tyler shot Jason a look. "So where are they? I dropped Melissa off at her office this afternoon and haven't heard from her since."

"Melissa rounded up Amy and their other friends for an emergency girl's night," he said. "I don't know what you did, but I hope it was good. She was pretty wound up when she stopped by Amy's earlier."

"Fucking perfect," Tyler muttered. "Wound up in a good way? Or pissed off?"

"Hell," Braden said with a chuckle. "Probably pissed off knowing you. But more importantly, does she have any single friends? If Tyler won't talk about it, you know it must be good."

"Their closest friends aren't single," Jason said, shaking his head. He gestured to the bartender for a beer, smirking. "One is married with twins, and the other is engaged."

"Well hell," Braden muttered. "Maybe she has a few hot realtor friends at the office. Think you can set me up, dude?"

"I'm not letting her introduce you to her friends," Tyler said, clutching his beer bottle as he took a long pull.

"Uh-huh. I'll just ask Melissa myself then."

The huge TV above the bar shifted to a newsbreak from the game that had been on, and Tyler frowned as he listened to the news anchor.

A woman in neighboring Prince William county is lucky to have escaped after nearly being kidnapped by a man she was showing properties to. Police will be releasing further information on the suspect later tonight. More details at 11:00.

"Fucking hell," Tyler said, clenching his fist.

"Jesus. That's probably the same guy as the BOLO we got on base," Braden said. "Wasn't another local realtor attacked or something recently?"

"You think it's the same guy?" Jason asked, raising his eyebrows.

"Why the hell not? Preying on female realtors? It sure sounds suspicious as hell," Tyler said, his gut churning. Melissa had said she had an open house to prepare for. What if the suspect in these most recent attacks showed up here? Or just walked into her office one day wanting to see some properties?

It wasn't too far-fetched for a criminal to move around within a local area.

To seek out new victims.

Briefly, his mind flashed back to the photographer lurking outside the home from over the weekend. Melissa seemed to trust him, but how well did she actually know him? Did she do some sort of background check on the people just worked with, or just trust them implicitly?

Braden frowned, looking over at them. "Does Melissa have any sort of weapon? And why'd they get a description of the suspect in the first incident and not this one?"

"Maybe he injured the victim, and she couldn't give a description. The news said she was nearly kidnapped."

"Fucking hell," Tyler muttered. "You think he attacked her?"

Jason shot him a pointed look.

Tyler's blood boiled, and he clenched his jaw. He wanted to race over to Melissa right now. Make sure she was safe, even though logically, he knew she was out with her friends. Surrounded by other people.

He wanted to take her back to his place and wrap her in his arms.

Hold her close where no one else could harm her.

Which was crazy.

She was out with her girlfriends, not alone in some open house. Not showing properties to a strange man. And besides, she wasn't his. Selling homes was her job. Her passion. She'd resent the hell out of him if he said she shouldn't do it anymore because it was unsafe.

Not that he had a say in her life anyway.

"Well?" Braden asked, looking at him.

"Well what?"

"Does she carry a weapon? Maybe she needs a

conceal carry permit."

"Hell," Tyler muttered. "I don't know if she even owns a gun. And I sure as hell won't encourage her to carry one unless she's been properly trained."

Jason glanced up at the TV as the game came back on. "I don't like this. Not for Melissa's sake or any of the other women. Amy likes to jog alone sometimes—her hours teaching preschool are totally different than mine on base. What if this guy just starts attacking random women?"

Tyler took a swig of his beer, the taste suddenly bitter in his mouth. "I don't like a damn thing about it either. No one around here is safe until he's caught."

Chapter 13

Melissa took a sip of her margarita, glancing around the table at her best friends. Music played over the speakers at the Mexican restaurant, bottles clinked behind the bar as drinks were prepared, and conversations carried on around them.

A waitress rushed by with a tray of steaming hot food, and her mouth began to water. How long had it been since she'd eaten? She'd gone out to the lake with Tyler and then been so worked up, so flushed and confused about everything, she'd skipped over a late lunch.

But now?

Surrounded by her best friends with a drink in her hand, she finally had her appetite back.

Beth dunked a chip in the salsa, popping it in her mouth. "All right, so what's the emergency? Did you run into Michael again or something?"

Melissa wrinkled her nose, frowning. "Thank God, no. And if I did, you'd probably be bailing me out of jail or something, not meeting me for Mexican."

"Wait, you ran into Michael? When?" Amy asked, her brown ponytail swinging back and forth as she glanced over at Melissa.

Melissa sighed. Her friends were focusing on the completely wrong thing. Not surprising, actually, since she'd gone on and on about breaking up with Michael forever. But now she had a new problem to worry about. A bigger concern than her ex.

And wasn't that a shock to her system.

"I saw him Saturday night after we met for drinks," she explained. "Tyler was walking me out to my car and there he was."

"Wait, who's Tyler?" Kara asked, glancing down distractedly at her phone. "Ugh, sorry. One of the twins is fussy. I might have to go call my husband."

Amy shot her a sympathetic look.

"Tyler is friends with Jason," Melissa said. "I was supposed to be meeting them for a drink, but then he decided to grace us with his presence."

"Another Marine?" Beth interrupted. "Did I know that detail?"

Melissa blew out an exasperated sigh, taking another sip of her margarita. "How should I know? I can barely keep track of my own life, let alone yours."

Beth laughed, taking a sip of her beer.

"All right ladies," their waitress said, setting the steaming hot tray of food down. "Here's your order. Sorry it's been so crazy tonight. Just one of those days." She served the women their entrees and then rushed off with the empty tray.

Melissa watched the steam rise from her cheese burrito, glancing back up at her friends. "Tyler is my newest client. Yes, he's friends with Jason. Yes, he's a

Marine. Yes, he helped me scare off Michael. But the actual point of tonight is that I went to the lake with him this afternoon."

"Wait, what?" Amy asked, pausing mid-bite of her taco to look over at her. "What lake? When?"

"Tyler came by my office to sign some paperwork. He talked me into going to this lake with him—it's kind of a long story. But, one thing led to another and—"

"You slept with him?" Beth asked, grinning. "I knew it."

"No! Not exactly. I mean, no, we didn't have sex. But we did fool around a little bit, and I just—it's crazy, right? I just called off my wedding! Well, I didn't, Michael did. Obviously. But this is just like a rebound thing, right? I mean I can't have feelings for a guy I just met."

"You think you have feelings for him?" Amy asked. "You two did seem pretty cozy the other night…."

"I don't know. Maybe." Melissa shrugged, brushing her hair back behind her shoulder. She adjusted her sweater, her mind flashing back to Tyler's lips on her bare skin. To his muscular arms wrapped around her. "I can't though, right? I mean I barely got over Michael. And Tyler and I do have this crazy chemistry between us—that's been evident since the first moment we met. But that's just lust, right?"

"Probably," Beth said. "Not that there's anything wrong with that."

Amy shushed her, glancing over at Melissa. "I knew with Jason right away that something was different about him. But I was in the same boat—too focused on my ex to give him a chance. I wasn't interested in dating at all."

"Well there's no way in hell that Michael and I would ever get back together. And after the way he treated me? I want absolutely zero to do with him. Ever."

"I don't blame you," Kara said, tucking her phone back into her purse. "The way he handled things was awful. It is a little ironic that you'd end up with another Marine though."

"I just—I feel like he gets me, which is weird. I barely know the guy, and we just click in a way that you don't always when you meet someone. I mean, shoot, some people I've known for years don't seem to understand me the way he already does. Which is insane!"

Amy's phone buzzed with a text, and glanced down at it and laughed. "Apparently Jason joined Tyler and some of the guys for a drink. It seems like you're on his mind, too."

"Yeah, I'm sure Tyler's the type to have a heart-to-heart with his closest Marine buddies," Melissa said sarcastically.

"Tyler was asking him about you."

Melissa felt heat surge through her. "I was feeling a little emotional at the lake and told him we had to leave. He didn't want to take me back to the office, though. I actually did have work to do. And I just can't even think straight sometimes when he's near."

"Did you hear about that realtor in the neighboring county?" Amy asked, suddenly looking concerned.

"Yeah, of course. She was nearly abducted. A friend of mine said she's in the hospital—that's why police haven't released a sketch of the suspect yet. I think they still need to interview her."

"How awful!" Amy gasped.

"It's horrible," Melissa agreed. "That's always a danger though when you're a woman, right? Everything could be a risk. I'm not going to live my life being afraid. I mean, what are the chances I'm next? Or that any of us are? It's a big world."

"I'd be careful," Beth advised. "I mean, I'm sure you already are, but until the guy is caught?"

Melissa shrugged. "There's not much that I can do. If I don't work, I won't earn commissions on sales. I've got to pay my mortgage and bills somehow."

"Hey," Beth said, looking thoughtful. "Did you ever find out more about your sister's fiancé?"

"Nope. He's still missing. I hate that she has to worry about it. It sounds like they sent in a team to look for them. It's possible they could be injured or captured. It's been a few days though. If they were taken hostage, I think they'd be telling the whole world."

"Agreed," Amy said. "That's exactly what Jason said."

"Part of me feels like I should fly out there and wait with her. But for how long, you know? We don't know anything, really. So if they find out something, then I'll go see her. She's going to class and trying to act like everything's normal. I'd just be sitting around her apartment if I went now."

"That's awful for her," Amy said. "And she's just finishing school, right?"

Melissa nodded, taking a bite of her cheese burrito. "I mean, maybe school is a good distraction.

Hopefully."

"So how's everything with Jason?" Beth asked, looking at Amy. "You seem pretty happy whenever you're together."

Amy flushed, a smile spreading across her face. "Good. Great, actually. We're still taking it slow. I mean, I think he'd love to move in together, but I'm not quite ready. He's over at my place all the time though."

"It works out well that you're right across the street from each other," Melissa said. "I mean that's almost like living together, except you can go back to your own place anytime you want."

"Well Tyler's looking to buy that big house, right?" Amy asked. "That's a surprise. I guess he's not staying in the Marines?"

"No, he wants to get out when this tour of duty is over. I think he plans to work at the Pentagon or something like that."

"How convenient," Beth joked, waggling her eyebrows. "You have the hots for a guy who's planning to stick around? Who's buying a home?"

"It's an investment," Melissa said, frowning.

"Uh-huh. Which is why every man stationed at Quantico is showing up at your office."

She rolled her eyes. "He's tired of moving around. I own a home, and I'm not looking to run off with the next man I meet."

"But you were engaged," Beth said. "I mean, I don't want to bring up bad memories, but I'm just saying—people who are more ready to settle down own houses."

Melissa's phone buzzed with a text, and she glanced down at it, her mouth dropping open in surprise when she saw Tyler's name flash across the screen.

I'm having drinks with my buddies, but all I can think about is you coming earlier.

Crying out my name.

You're fucking gorgeous, Melissa.

She flushed, feeling heat rise within her.

"Whoa," Beth said with a laugh. "Is that from Tyler or something? Because I don't think I've ever seen you blush before."

"God, he's incorrigible," she muttered, thumbing a response.

Don't start sending me dick pics or something.

Her phone buzzed with his reply.

Wouldn't dream of it.

But if you want to send me naked pics, I wouldn't be opposed.

For my eyes only.

She rolled her eyes. Yeah right.

Don't count on it.

Tyler responded immediately.

Don't worry. Every time I close my eyes, I can see those gorgeous breasts of yours.

Taste them.

She flushed again, remembering his mouth on her nipples. His tongue flickering against the taut buds. Holy hell. The man hadn't even fully undressed her, and she'd gone up in flames. She'd been achy and needy all afternoon, despite him making her come.

And there was no way she was admitting that to him.

She took a sip of her margarita, trying to clear her head.

Her phone buzzed once again.

Let me know when I can see you again.

That was just the crux of it, wasn't it? She wasn't sure if she should see him again. Not in anything other than a professional sense, at least. She didn't trust herself when they were together. Didn't trust that she wouldn't do something she'd regret in the morning.

Didn't trust that she wouldn't fall hard.

She looked back up at her friends, already engaged in another conversation. In a way, Michael had ruined that for her. Her chance of happiness. Her ability to trust that a man wouldn't hurt her again.

A fling with Tyler wouldn't lead her anywhere she wanted—no matter how attracted to him she was.

Going down that road would lead to nothing but heartache once more.

Chapter 14

Melissa jerked awake as her phone buzzed from across the room on her dresser, fumbling in her sheets. She kicked off the twisted covers and blinked in the darkness, finally glancing over at her alarm clock on the nightstand.

Three a.m.

She rose and stumbled across the room, picking up her cell phone to see her sister's name flashing on the screen. Her heart lurched into her throat as she swiped at the phone, blinking at it with blurry eyes, trying to answer the call.

"Becky! What's wrong? Did they find Brody?" she asked, nearly dropping the phone in her haste.

"They found him! Oh my God, they found him. He's injured, and they're airlifting him to a hospital somewhere. I'm still trying to find out more information. But he's alive, and that's all that matters right now."

"Oh my God, that's unbelievable!" Melissa

shrieked. "They seriously found him?"

"Yeah, his commander just called me. I still don't know what happened. Hopefully they'll let me fly out there to see him. I don't even know how long it will be before he can be flown back stateside."

"So he's going to be okay?" Melissa asked, breathing a sigh of relief. "Oh my God, this is unbelievable."

"I don't know. I don't know anything about the extent of his injuries. It's just—after he's been missing—" She choked up, letting out a relieved sob.

"Becky, oh God. Do you want me to come with you?"

"No, I'll be fine," she said, sniffling. "These are happy tears right now, I swear. I'm not even sure if I'm allowed to visit him. I think it's a military hospital somewhere. I'm just focusing on the good now—the positive. He's alive, and that's all that matters. I'll deal with everything else later."

Melissa paced back and forth across her bedroom, her eyes adjusting to the darkness. "So who called you? His commander? This is so crazy! He's been missing for days."

"I know, I know. I'd totally assumed the worst at this point. Especially with no real updates and—"

Her voice cut off again, and Melissa's chest clenched. "Understandable. I'm in shock, too." She sank down onto her bed, clutching her hand to her chest. Her heart was racing, and she didn't know whether to laugh or cry. She was just so relieved Brody had been found. So in shock over the whole thing. "Let me know when you're flying out to see him. I want to know details, flight info, everything. And if you need anything at all—plane tickets, hotel reservations, whatever, you let me know."

"I will. I promise I'll let you know as soon as I have more information. I just found out a few minutes ago and had to call you right away. God, I'm sorry, I know it's the middle of the night on the East coast. I just couldn't wait until morning."

"It's fine," Melissa assured her. "Are you kidding me? Of course I'd want to know right away! I've got a slow day tomorrow anyway. I've got an open house this weekend and some stuff to prep for, but tomorrow I can sleep in and relax."

"Okay. Well I'll let you get back to bed. I just—I just can't believe it, you know?"

"I do know. Wow. It's like he's gotten a second chance or something. Call me the second you find out anything else, promise?"

"Yeah, I promise."

"I love you," Melissa said into the phone.

"I love you, too. Goodnight."

Melissa said goodbye and ended the call, setting the phone right on her nightstand instead of usually where she kept it across the room. She liked to leave it there with her backup alarm, in case she had trouble getting up in the mornings. There was no way she could shut it off without getting up and crossing her bedroom.

But now?

She wanted it beside her to grab immediately. She needed to be able to grab it the instant her sister called again.

Lying back down in her bed, she knew she'd never be able to fall back asleep right away. She was too wound up. Too agitated. Tomorrow morning couldn't get here soon enough.

***

Melissa pulled into the parking lot of her office at eleven the next morning, a cup of steaming hot coffee in her hand. She shut off the engine and climbed out of her vehicle, clicking the remote to lock her SUV before walking across the lot toward the front door.

Her stilettos clicked on the asphalt, and she caught her reflection in the glass door—long red hair flowing over her wool coat, shapely legs in her sky-high stilettos.

Not bad. If only Tyler were around to see—

"Excuse me!" a man called out.

She glanced over to see a guy of around fifty or so hurrying her way. He was dressed in neat khakis and a button-down shirt, beneath a long wool coat that hung open. His graying hair was slicked back, but he had a warm smile on his face.

"Can I help you?" she asked, pausing.

"I'm wondering if Mary is in the office? She was supposed to show me a property today."

"Oh," Melissa said, nodding. "I'm sorry, but she has today off. Maybe you got your times mixed up or something? She's usually in and out of the office but had an appointment today."

"Shoot," the man said, coming closer. He slipped off his sunglasses, his bright blue eyes gazing at her. "I don't suppose anyone else could show me the property? I've got a business trip this afternoon and will be gone for the next week. I don't want to miss out if this is my chance to get an offer in."

"I might be able to take you there," she said, turning toward the door. "Let me give her a call."

"I'm in kind of a hurry, actually. Is there any chance we could head over there now?"

Melissa glanced back toward him, pressing her mouth together. Rushing off with a client would throw a wrench in her plans for the day. Still, Mary had helped her out occasionally when she had multiple buyers looking to move on a home. She wouldn't steal the sale from her or anything, just show this man the property before he caught his flight. Then Mary could deal with putting in an offer if that's what he decided.

"What's the address?" she asked.

"I have it here in my phone," he said, flashing her a warm smile as he pulled his cell from his pocket.

Melissa's phone buzzed in her bag, and she excused herself for a moment, grabbing it. "Are we all set to take the photos later on?" she asked the photographer, praying he wasn't going to go into one of his lengthy phone chats.

"Yes, I just wanted to confirm the time. And see if you needed me to pick up anything on the way over?"

Melissa resisted the urge to roll her eyes. "No, I'm good. And I'll meet you there at two as planned. You have the address?"

"Yes, absolutely. I'll see you then."

"Do you have an appointment later?" the man asked as she tucked her phone back into her bag. "I don't want to take up your time if someone's expecting you."

"Not until two, so we should have plenty of time. Let me know the address and we can head over to see it."

"Fantastic." He recited the address to her, and Melissa pulled her keys back from her bag, taking a sip of her coffee.

"I can drive," he insisted. "I'll drop you back off here on my way to the airport."

"Where are you flying out of?"

"Dulles. We can make this quick, and then I'll head up to Dulles to catch my flight. My suitcase is already in the trunk. I was hoping to squeeze this in."

"Understandable," she said, walking in front of him as he gestured for her to go ahead on the sidewalk. She took another sip of her coffee, mentally tallying the list of things she'd need to do when she returned to the office.

"I'm just around the corner," he said.

She frowned, wondering why he wouldn't have parked in the front lot. A few cars sped by on the main road, but a moment later, it was just the two of them walking in front of the building. She paused, beginning to rethink driving with him. She could head over in her SUV, show him the property, and send him on his way.

Call Mary from the car and let her know she was showing the property to her client.

She paused, pulling her phone from her bag, and suddenly the man was right behind her, one arm pinning her arms in place as he pulled her against him. Her coffee fell to the ground, spilling over her stilettos and burning her skin. She let out a small shriek, a foul-smelling cloth covering her nose and mouth, and she struggled, trying to pull away.

"That's it, darling," he said, tightening his grip as he pinned her against him. "Breathe deep. There's nowhere to run."

She struggled harder, her vision beginning to blur, and he held the cloth to her face. If she could just pull away. Just call 911 or Tyler. Just scream for help.

She sagged against her attacker as the world faded to black.

Chapter 15

Tyler drummed his fingers on his desk, restless. He scanned through the document open on his computer for the third time, the words barely registering. He still didn't have a clue what the damn report was about. Still couldn't concentrate on a thing.

His gaze landed on his cell phone.

Still no word from Melissa.

No answer to his texts, no wisecrack about him being a jackass.

Nothing.

When Jason had told him earlier that her sister's missing boyfriend—scratch that, fiancé—had been found? He'd sent her another string of texts.

And still—radio silence.

Was Melissa upset about his taking her down to the lake yesterday? About him kissing her and stripping off her sweater in his SUV? He hadn't exactly planned to move that quickly with her, but she hadn't seemed upset about what had happened. And according to Jason, all had been good with the women last night.

They'd supposedly all left in high spirits.

He grabbed the phone on his desk, dialing the number for Jason's office on the floor below his. Jason answered on the second ring.

"I haven't been able to get ahold of Melissa all morning," Tyler said, clearing his throat. "Did she fly out to see her sister or something?"

"That's a negative," Jason said. "I know she called Amy before she headed off to teach preschool. As far as I know, she had a full day planned at the office. I think she would've told her if she was catching a flight."

Tyler clenched his fist. Maybe she was just ignoring him. Just busy and she hadn't gotten a chance to text him back yet.

Worry niggled at the back of his mind though.

Melissa usually always had her phone with her and was quick to shoot him a text reply. Even if she was calling him an ass, she'd always texted back. Something was up. "I might swing by her office."

"You think something's wrong?" Jason asked, sounding surprised. "I know there's been a lot of stuff on the news lately, but she's got a lot going on with her sister right now. She might just be busy this afternoon."

"Understood. I'd just feel better seeing for myself. It's not like her to not respond at all."

"I'll call Amy and see if she's heard anything. She might be tough to get a hold of since she's teaching right now, but I'll see if I can get someone to go down to her classroom and have her call me."

"I appreciate it," Tyler said. "Doesn't she have her

cell?"

"She leaves it off during class."

"Roger that. I'll talk to you later."

He hung up the phone and was rising from his desk before he could think about it. Locking his computer screen and palming his keys. Although Melissa was probably fine, he needed to see her. Hear her voice. Touch her.

He'd feel better when he was certain that she was okay.

***

Twenty minutes later, he was pulling into the lot of her real estate office. He spotted her SUV in the parking lot and let out a breath he hadn't even realized that he'd been holding.

She was here.

Perfectly safe.

He felt a little paranoid rushing over for no reason, but he might as well go see her now that he'd arrived. Maybe even give her a hard time for not texting him back. He strode across the lot, frowning as he saw the photographer from the other day looking in the window of her vehicle. What was it with this guy?

Why was he always prowling around?

"Hey!" Tyler said loudly, storming over.

The man jumped, relaxing slightly when he recognized Tyler. "Oh, it's you. Have you heard from Ms. Ford?" he asked. "I haven't been able to get ahold of her."

"No, I just came by to check on her. What the hell are you doing peeking in the windows of her car?"

"I was supposed to meet her," the man said,

frowning. "We had an appointment for two o'clock. We even spoke on the phone earlier, confirming it. She didn't show and wasn't answering her phone, so I came here. It's not like her to miss an appointment like that."

"Shit," Tyler muttered, glancing around. "I haven't been able to get ahold of her either."

"Well, her car's here, so that's something. Maybe she just got tied up with something in the office."

"I don't like it," Tyler said, turning and striding toward the front door. The photographer hurried along behind him, and then Tyler was yanking the glass door open and storming inside. The young receptionist looked up in surprise, and Tyler halted at her desk. "Where's Melissa?" he asked bluntly. "She missed an appointment and isn't returning any calls."

The receptionist peered around him, glancing out the window. "I assumed she was here," she said, looking bewildered. "That's her car out front."

"Go check her office," Tyler commanded. "Check the ladies' room. No one has seen or heard from her in several hours."

"Right, of course," the receptionist said, standing up and hurrying off.

"It's not like her to miss an appointment," the photographer said again. "She's never late either. Maybe she's sick or there was some sort of emergency."

"Yeah, she gave me hell for being late the other day," Tyler muttered. "What could've happened to her?" He glanced out the window, his gaze sweeping the lot. There had to be security cameras around with all the local businesses. Some cars might even have dash cams. If someone was driving by, they might've seen something.

But what?

People didn't just disappear out of thin air. Had she been showing a home? No, probably not since her vehicle was here. But what if she went with someone?

Tyler leaned over the desk of the receptionist, flipping through the papers stacked there. What he expected to find, he didn't know. Each realtor probably kept their own schedule and showed homes as they came on the market. As their clients showed interest.

They set up appointments and kept their own schedule.

There wasn't some master schedule that listed everything.

"I don't see her anywhere," the receptionist said, walking back. "I've checked the conference rooms, break room, bathroom.... I assume you've tried calling her?"

"Hell yes," Tyler said, clenching his fist in frustration. "Calling, texting. I drove over here from Quantico. What time did she get in this morning?"

"She was expected around eleven. I can check with IT and see if she logged into her computer. Or we can try calling her house, but her car's still here...."

"No, I think she did arrive around eleven," the photographer said. "That's when I called her. She was just arriving at the office, and we confirmed our appointment for this afternoon."

Tyler nodded, glancing around. "So we'll see when she logged in. Obviously she didn't leave in her own vehicle. But if she was showing properties, she could've come in and left with someone else. Maybe she pulled up a property listing or something. We can go check there."

The receptionist glanced down at her papers. "I don't have a record of that. If she came in, she would've notified me. At least gotten a copy of a driver's license for a new client. And if she already had something scheduled first thing, I don't know why she'd come here first."

"Fuck," Tyler muttered. "I'm going to look around outside."

He pushed open the front door and walked back into the parking lot, frowning at the snow flurries. Damn wonderful. Yesterday the weather was beautiful, and today it was full on winter again. At least they weren't expecting a major storm or some shit like that.

He looked around the lot again, his gaze tracking over the few vehicles, before turning back toward the real estate office. He glanced down the sidewalk, his chest clenching as he saw a spilled cup of coffee on the ground a few storefronts down.

Jogging down the sidewalk, his heart stopped as he spotted Melissa's crushed cell phone beside it. Someone had thrown her coffee to the ground and stomped on the screen of her phone, cracking it. Rendering it useless.

Someone had taken her. Grabbed her things and snatched her right from the parking light. Right in the middle of the day.

"God damn it!" he shouted as the photographer and receptionist came running out the front door.

Tyler pulled out his phone, dialing 911 as his heart pounded. He clutched his phone so hard it dug into the skin of his hand as the operator answered the call.

"911, what's your emergency?" a female voice asked.

"I need to report a kidnapping."

Chapter 16

Tyler paced back and forth in Jason's living room, agitated. He clenched his fists, his blood boiling as his mind raced through a million possible scenarios. A million different ways Melissa could be hurt. A million different places she could be.

He grabbed his phone from his pocket, staring at the blank screen.

Willing for it to ring. For Melissa to text him, saying this had all been a big misunderstanding.

Impossible since they'd found her crushed phone, but hell.

How could so many hours have gone by with no new information?

Why hadn't the police found her yet?

It didn't seem possible.

Not her missing, not the fact that they had no idea where she was. None of it.

Amy sat on the sofa, sobbing, with Jason trying to comfort her as the other men from base huddled together and made calls.

"Call me back as soon as you know anything," Braden angrily said into his cell phone, slamming it down on the coffee table in frustration. "The damn police won't tell me anything," he muttered. "No updates, no possibilities about her location, nothing."

"Me either," Tyler muttered. "And every minute that's she gone is another minute that someone could be harming her. Hurting her. Taking her farther away from us. Every minute matters, and they won't tell us a God damn thing!"

"How can she be gone?" Amy wailed. "This doesn't make any sense. She's always so careful! She's been in real estate forever, and she's always careful. Always." She sniffled again, Jason grabbing her some more tissues from the coffee table.

"She let her guard down," Tyler said, his gut clenching. "She was happy about her sister, up early this morning from the sounds of it. And when she got to work, she must've thought she was meeting with an actual client."

"But why would she go off with someone like that? That video shows a man walking up to her in front of her real estate office, and then she just leaves with him! And we have no idea what happened!"

Tyler nodded, feeling bile churn in his stomach.

The police had showed them a surveillance video, asking if any of them could identify the man she was last seen with. By all accounts, he'd never been there before. No one recognized him. No one knew him. None of his information was on file.

Which meant that Melissa thought it was someone she could trust.

Did she think he was someone else? Had he lied

and made up some story?

Fucking hell.

"We don't know," Jason said in a low voice. "Maybe she thought she knew him. Or he could've lied and told her anything. It looks like she left with him willingly."

"Or started to," Amy said bitterly. "We don't know what happened when they went offscreen."

"The police are looking for additional surveillance footage," Tyler said. "There could always be other witnesses. Hell, if everything weren't closed, I'd be down there right now asking people what they saw."

Liam looked up from his laptop. "It seemed like it took them a damn long time to show us the surveillance footage. What the hell were they doing all afternoon?"

"They might've been reviewing it themselves," Jason said. "Seeing if they could get a hit off of facial recognition or something."

"Did they ever release the description of the suspect in the other attempted kidnapping from the other day?"

"I'll look it up and see," Liam said, typing quickly on his laptop.

"I don't think so," Braden said. "Which makes me wonder if this is the same guy. If they know who it is, maybe they're closing in on him. Maybe they don't want it all over the news."

"Damn it," Tyler said, punching his fist into his open hand. "I hate just sitting here doing nothing. Melissa could be hurt. Scared out of her mind. Just sitting back and doing nothing is killing me."

"The police are trained for this," Jason said. "Maybe we're Marines trained in war, but we're not used to sweeping scenes of kidnappings."

"Shit," Tyler muttered.

"I called her sister," Amy said, wiping away her tears. "I felt awful doing so—she just found out her fiancé was alive. And now her sister's been kidnapped? I couldn't just not tell her though."

"It's a fucked-up world," Tyler muttered.

"Cool it," Jason chastised him.

"It's fine," Amy said. "He has every right to be upset. Melissa is missing! My God, we have no idea where she is or if she'll be okay. I just saw her last night, but what if I never see her again?" Fresh tears rolled down her cheeks, and Jason pulled her close.

"So what the hell are we supposed to do all night?" Tyler asked, frustration surging through him. He was a man of action. Not someone used to sitting around, waiting for updates.

"We wait," Jason said, shooting him a look. "We stay here until we get word. That's the best thing we can do for her right now."

Chapter 17

Melissa groaned as she opened her eyes, blinking in the darkness. Her wrists and ankles were tightly bound, and she was curled up in a cramped space. The trunk of a car, she realized as she felt the car she was riding in lurch.

Oh God, they were driving somewhere.

Waves of nausea rolled over her, threatening to make her sick all over the trunk.

Snippets of memory came rushing back.

The man.

The parking lot.

Offering to show him the house.

She'd turned to get her keys from her bag, and he'd grabbed her. The polite-looking middle aged guy, dressed in business clothes, not some scruffy loner. Not a big guy covered in tattoos who stood out anywhere he went.

This guy had looked…harmless. Normal. He'd said he was there to see Mary, another one of the realtors.

And then the second she'd let her guard down, he'd grabbed her.

She wracked her brain trying to think if anyone else had been around. If other cars had been in the lot. If other customers had been in the shops nearby.

Someone had to have seen something, right? And if not, there were surveillance cameras there. Traffic cams. Something, anything, that would show this guy driving into the parking lot.

That would show her SUV arrive and never leave.

But what if he'd taken her car? He could've been working with someone. Could've thrown her in his own trunk and then moved her vehicle. This man could've driven her SUV off to God knows where, and no one would have been the wiser.

What if no one even realized that she was missing?

Tears pooled in her eyes as her muscles cramped. Her wrists hurt from how tightly they'd been bound, but at least they were in front of her. If her arms had been behind her back, she'd really have felt helpless.

Her stomach churned as the car turned a corner, and she squeezed her eyes shut, taking a few deep breaths.

Her sister had probably tried to call her back to give her updates about Brody. She might realize something was wrong. And she'd never returned Tyler's text last night. Sure he'd been fantasizing about their afternoon together, but he had asked when he could see her again.

And she'd been so confused about the whole situation she hadn't even responded. Just left that text there on her phone, waiting, while she'd continued her night out with her friends. He'd been with the guys, too, from what Amy had said.

Oh God.

What if she never saw him again either?

What if this man attacked her when they arrived wherever they were going—raped her? Killed her?

She gasped as tears began to roll down her cheeks. Blinking away the dampness, she took a shuddering breath. Willed herself to calm down.

Had they been driving all this time?

Should she scream? Or was it better not to let him know that she was awake?

She listened, trying to hear the sounds of traffic around them. To hear voices. People. Anything.

They could be anywhere by now.

Shoot, maybe she wasn't even with the man who'd grabbed her. He could've been working with anyone.

The car slowed slightly, and she realized she could see the brake lights from inside the trunk if she twisted her head. One little light was all that stood between her and the rest of the world.

Weren't there emergency releases on the insides of trunks?

If she could twist and turn around, maybe she could move enough to release it. Lift up her arms and grab it or nudge it somehow. Why hadn't she ever looked in her own trunk before? Sure, it was probably different in an SUV, but wasn't that something she should pay attention to?

Throwing her body to one side, she smacked her head against the back of the vehicle. With a lot of wiggling and frustration, she finally managed to turn herself so that she was facing the back of the vehicle. She lifted her bound wrists, fumbling in the darkness.

A car honked behind them, and as the car she was

in pulled forward again, she realized this was her chance. Someone was around. Someone would see her.

Kicking as hard as she could at the brake lights, she screamed.

She grabbed onto something with numb hands and tried to open the trunk. Tried to free herself.

Kicking harder and harder, she finally kicked out the entire brake light. The car behind them honked again and again. A siren sounded from nearby, and she kept kicking and fumbling in the darkness, sobbing.

The car she was in sped up and swerved, and she screamed as she was thrown around the back of the trunk. They suddenly swerved off the road, and as her head hit the top of the trunk, everything faded to blackness.

Chapter 18

"They found her!" Jason shouted, holding the phone away from his mouth as he yelled out to the group in his living room. "It's someone from down at the precinct. They found her, and she's on her way to the hospital now."

Tyler was on his feet in an instant, sliding his cell phone into his back pocket. Pulling out his keys.

"What hospital?" he demanded. "Where is she?"

Jason spoke into the phone in a low voice, Tyler's heart racing. Wherever she was, whatever had happened, she was okay. They'd deal with it together. As long as he got to see her again and hold her safe in his arms, right where she belonged, they'd both be okay.

Jason put down his phone and looked around the room. "They're up near Arlington. She was kidnaped and put in the trunk of a vehicle. They drove her up there and around for a couple of hours."

"Fucking hell," Tyler spat out.

"She kicked out the brake lights, apparently. The police here were already searching the suspect's home after surveillance footage showed his vehicle. They traced the plates and got his address. A local police officer saw the car driving erratically and the brake light gone. He pulled them over and found her in the trunk."

Amy began sobbing on the sofa, and Jason sank back down beside her, wrapping her in his arms.

Tyler's stomach churned as he thought about how frightened she must have been. She was so damn smart to kick out the brake lights. Melissa was a fighter and wouldn't let anyone or anything get her down. "She's at Arlington hospital?" he asked.

"Affirmative. They said only family can see her but—"

"Like fucking hell I won't see her."

Tyler was out the door and running to his SUV a moment later. Revving the engine and peeling out of the quiet little neighborhood that Jason and Amy lived in. At this time of night, he could be on 95 and up in Arlington in less than an hour.

Every minute away from Melissa had felt like an eternity, but she was safe. His.

He'd known something was wrong earlier instinctively.

As crazy and fast as things had happened, he knew her. He was already falling in love with her.

He wasn't going to let her run from him.

To let her fear of being in a relationship prevent them from being together.

Nearly losing her had shown him just how much she meant to him. Just how much they were meant to be together. They'd take their time getting to know each other more, sure. To build on what they'd started.

But he already knew that he couldn't live without her.

***

Tyler hurried down the stark white hallway of the hospital, adrenaline pumping through him. He'd had to sweet talk the nurses to let him see Melissa tonight, but flashing his military ID had helped smooth the way somewhat.

He eased open the door to her room in case she was sleeping, and his chest clenched as he saw her lying there in a hospital gown. Her red hair lay flowing around her, and with her pale skin, she looked so fragile.

Breakable.

The thin blanket that covered her looked like it wouldn't offer her any warmth at all, and he was already shrugging out of his jacket, ready to lay it across her as she slept.

Melissa turned her head as he quietly slid into the room, and then she was crying. Calling for him.

Tyler rushed to her side, anger coursing through him as he saw the dark circles under her eyes. The red marks around her wrists as she reached for him.

"Beautiful," he said, his voice cracking as he draped his jacket over her.

"Tyler, oh God. I didn't think I'd see you again," she said as he held her cold hands and then ran one of his own gently over her bare arm. "I was so scared."

"Of course you'd see me again," he soothed,

gently brushing his fingers over her temple. "You're a fighter. You fought and you escaped."

"I just—I was so stupid. That guy said he was meeting another realtor—I don't even know if he knew her! He could've just looked up our names on the website. And when he parked around the corner, I decided to drive separately and was getting my keys, and then he grabbed me!"

She choked out a sob as tears ran down her face, and Tyler's chest clenched.

He hated seeing her crying. Hated seeing her helpless and scared.

"But you fought, beautiful. You were smart and strong and escaped. You found yourself in a bad situation, and you didn't give up. You fought and helped the police find you." He wiped her tears away, his eyes running over her body to check for any other injuries.

"Did he—were you—?" He cut himself off, not even able to say the words.

She gasped, pulling her hands free from his grip to wipe away her tears. "He didn't hurt me. He knocked me out and put me in the trunk—tied me up. God knows what would've happened if the police didn't stop him."

Tyler cleared his throat. "Apparently they were already searching his house. Surveillance footage showed you talking with him in front of your office. The police were able to get a license plate from the car he was driving. I guess there was other footage of him driving around the parking lot."

"What time is it anyway? It feels like days have passed. I'm so exhausted."

"Eleven p.m.," Tyler said. "He grabbed you earlier

and apparently drove around for a damn long time. We're not sure why. What do you remember about what happened?"

"Not much," she said. "He grabbed me out front, and the next thing I remember is waking up bound in a trunk. I didn't know what has happening, and when I realized?" Her voice cut off again as she choked back a sob.

"I'm so sorry, beautiful," Tyler said. "That never should've happened to you. Never. Thank God that bastard is behind bars, because I would fucking end him."

"And you came to me," she whispered, tears smarting her eyes again. "I was scared and alone, and you came."

"Of course I came. Where else would I be?" he asked in a low voice. "I was worried out of my mind about you."

"I was so scared I'd never see you again. And I never texted you back yesterday—I was just overwhelmed by everything. By us. I didn't expect to feel anything for you, and then in your SUV—"

He took her hand, hating the scared look on her face. "I'm not going anywhere, gorgeous. However long you need is fine with me. I'm in no hurry. I already told you that you're safe with me, and I meant it. It's crazy that it's so fast, but I'm falling in love with you, Melissa."

Tears streamed down her cheeks. "I'm falling in love with you, too."

Epilogue

Three Weeks Later

"Why'd you want to come here?" Tyler asked as they drove in his SUV down toward the same lake he'd taken her to a few weeks earlier. "Not that I mind, I'm just curious."

Melissa glanced over at him, smiling. "It just felt like this was where everything started with us."

He smirked, his green eyes flashing with amusement. "That it did, beautiful." His gaze raked over her before he turned back to the road. "And I'm glad you still have another week off work. I kind of like having you all to myself."

She flushed, thinking of Tyler's arms wrapped around her every night. Of waking up next to him every morning. Although he'd held her and they'd kissed for hours, they'd otherwise been taking things slowly. Her physical injuries had been minor, fortunately, but it had taken a little time for her to feel comfortable in her own skin again.

And Tyler had been perfectly happy with holding her close.

"And what are you going to do when you settle on your house?" she teased. "Leave me alone in my bed every night?"

"I'll sweet talk you into spending the night at my place some of the time," he said with a chuckle. "And if I need to move? Luckily I know a good realtor."

"It'll be good to get back to work," she said with a contented sigh. "I mean, I can't let you close on your house without me there."

He reached over and grabbed her hand, his thick fingers interlocking with hers. "I'm just glad you're all right," he said in a low voice. "The house doesn't matter. Just us."

"Just us," she agreed.

They pulled into the clearing, coming to a stop right by the lake where they'd been before. The sun glistened off the water, and a few birds flew through the air. "We should come here when the weather's warmer," she said. "It must be gorgeous in the spring."

"Yep," he agreed. "But I'm happy coming here anytime as long as you're with me."

She looked over at him and smiled, her gaze roaming over his chiseled features.

"Come here," he said, pushing his seat back and hauling her into his arms. "I want you close."

She tugged the sweater dress she had on up slightly higher on her thighs and eagerly settled on his lap, smiling. His broad hands landed on her hips, and his lips quirked. "I like this better than the jeans you had on last time."

"I thought you might say that," she said.

He ducked down and kissed her, his lips hot and hungry against her own. "I'm in no hurry, beautiful. We can wait as long as you need."

"I'm not wearing any panties," she teased, loving the quick intake of his breath.

"Don't tease a guy like that, beautiful," he said, raising a hand to lightly caress one breast through her sweater dress.

"Who said I'm teasing?"

He claimed her mouth once more, and then she was softly moaning as he lightly bucked against her. "I'm not making love to you for the first time in my car," he muttered.

"Why not?" she asked lightly. "We're starting over. Right now." She reached down between them, unbuckling his belt, and then Tyler was suddenly taking over. Pushing her dress up to her waist. Baring her to him. Running his fingers through her silken folds, groaning in approval.

She gasped as his thick fingers dragged through her arousal-dampened folds, lightly circling her clit.

"God, you're so wet for me, beautiful. So ready."

She gasped as he circled her clit again, swearing she began to see stars. She clutched onto his shoulders, crying out as he growled in approval.

Tyler pulled his erection free, and then he quickly sheathed himself and was lowering her atop him. Claiming her once and for all as his.

She gasped as his hot, hard length filled her. As he bottomed out deep inside, the exquisite pressure nearly too much to bear.

"You okay, beautiful?" he asked, pausing a moment.

"God yes, don't stop."

His mouth was on hers again, and she moved atop him, riding him. Surrendering as he again took control. The base of his erection rubbed up against her clit with every thrust, and she moaned, unable to stop the waves of pleasure taking over.

He easily lifted her up and down even as he bucked into her, and then she closed her eyes, crying out as she reached the precipice.

With one more powerful thrust, she was coming. Screaming his name.

Claimed utterly and completely by him.

Tyler hardened and then found his release as well, groaning in pleasure.

She gazed up into his green eyes, breathless and spent, as his arms tightened around her. He kissed her once, twice, holding her close. "I love you, gorgeous."

"I love you, too."

About the Author

Makenna Jameison is a bestselling romance author. She writes military romance and romantic suspense with hot alpha males, steamy scenes, and happily-ever-afters.

Her debut series made it to #1 in Romance Short Stories on Amazon. Makenna loves the beach, strong coffee, red wine, and traveling. She lives in Washington DC with her husband and two daughters.

Visit www.makennajameison.com to discover your next great read.

Made in the USA
Columbia, SC
09 June 2025

59169001R00098